WHO SHOT YA

RENTA

RENTA

Lock Down Publications and
Ca$h Presents
Who Shot Ya
A Novel by Renta

RENTA

Lock Down Publications
P.O. Box 870494
Mesquite, Tx 75187

Visit our website
www.lockdownpublications.com

Copyright 2018 by Who Shot Ya Renta

Lock Down Publications
Like our page on Facebook: Lock Down Publications
@
www.facebook.com/lockdownpublications.ldp
Cover design and layout by: **Dynasty Cover Me**
Book interior design by: **Shawn Walker**
Edited by: **Lashonda Johnson**

4

Stay Connected with Us!

Text **LOCKDOWN** to 22828 to stay up-to-date with new releases, sneak peeks, contests and more…

Submission Guideline.

Submit the first three chapters of your completed manuscript to ldpsubmissions@gmail.com, subject line: Your book's title. The manuscript must be in a .doc file and sent as an attachment. The document should be in Times New Roman, double-spaced and in size 12 font. Also, provide your synopsis and full contact information. If sending multiple submissions, they must each be in a separate email.

Have a story but no way to send it electronically? You can still submit to LDP/Ca$h Presents. Send in the first three chapters, written or typed, of your completed manuscript to:

LDP: Submissions Dept
Po Box 870494
Mesquite, Tx 75187

DO NOT send original manuscript. Must be a duplicate.

Provide your synopsis and a cover letter containing your full contact information.

Thanks for considering LDP and Ca$h Presents.

Acknowledgments

I hail from the mud. I heard it was beauty in the struggle, but the blocks I come from created monsters outta innocence. Ain't no beauty in that, I salute the fam. I ain't got too many, yet the few I do have, the love is pure. I owe y'all the world. When I fight for a breath to breathe, y'all do CPR. When I'm on my other shit, y'all blow me off and do shit to get me right.

Only when it's real, mayne! Cash and the LDP, fam, what's up? I honestly don't know how far this pen will take me, but just for the opportunity to see, I salute the squad. At times I don't know if God is listening. If He said 'fuck me' or if I am talking to the wind, but just in case, I'm still trying to understand.

Either or good lookin' my, 'G'. I owe you one. Moose I ain't gotta say it, at times like this, I just hope you can see me. To my readers, I do it for y'all.

RENTA

Chapter One
Free My Mu'Fuckin' Brother

Sweat dripped from his forehead as Nutz crouched outside of Destiny Kendricks' red brick home. The bushes concealing him made a good cover as he awaited her arrival. He'd been camouflaged behind those bushes for at least four hours. Yet, four hours held no measure compared to his crooked intentions. Darkness had fallen upon the tainted streets of Denton, Texas, and the four lines of the *white* he'd indulged earlier had him anxious. As well as prepared to execute whoever, and whatever dared come between him and his brother's reunion.

"Fuck this bitch at?" he wondered out loud.

As if God had heard the frustrations lacing his voice, headlights from a gray Dodge Charger, illuminated the exterior of the four-bedroom house. A crazed smile touched his lips as he screwed the silencer onto the P.89.

"Showtime," he whispered.

He observed intently as Destiny unknowingly strolled right past the bushes where potential death sat, awaiting the right moment to monopolize. She was fumbling with her keys, trying to balance the bag of groceries on her hip, while inserting the key into the lock, all at once. A woman's intuition is the feminine attribute of a man's instinct and ten times more powerful. As if Destiny could sense Nutz presence, she nervously glanced around.

"Damn, I wish Sa'Mage hurry up and bring his ass home," she said aloud.

Destiny turned back to the door finally getting it open. Just as God allowed her this small blessing the devil appeared in the form of a gangsta. Fear suddenly gripped her as she felt the muzzle against the back of her neck, causing her to inhale

9

deeply and freeze on impact. Nutz slid closely behind her and began whispering his reasons for invading her place of safety.

Nutz aggressively grabbed a handful of her hair. "Dig this, sweetheart. My beef ain't with you, feel me? I don't intend to harm you, but if you go against the grain, I'll push your next thoughts through your forehead." Nutz used the barrel of his gun to emphasize his point. Then he ran it down her pretty face. Fear vibrated through her body as he brought his lips' inches from her ear. "Me and your pussy ass husband got some bidness to 'tend to. Since I know, you're the Queen of the board—" He ran his tongue over her ear, then continued. "I must snatch you up to see if he's the type of playa, that depends on his Queen to win. Or is he as heartless as I am and can play without his most powerful piece? I'm gonna ask you right now can you follow instructions, love?"

Destiny struggled against him and inhaled deeply. Nutz jammed the barrel into the side of her face, so hard it broke the skin, and a small tear of blood ran down her face.

Urine escaped from Destiny as she lost control of her facilities. Tears formed and fell from her eyes as the realization of her predicament set in. She nodded her head in confirmation. Nutz brought his face inches from her neck. She could feel his warm breath on her perspiring flesh, as her body shook from sobbing.

"Let's hope your boy loves you enough to lie under oath," Nutz hissed.

Destiny's mouth was suddenly covered with a wet cloth. She held her breath trying not to inhale the odorless gas until her lungs screamed for oxygen.

"Just breathe, mama. It will be over before you know it. Destiny was still fighting not to inhale. "Damn, just relax mane." He sang in her ear and as she continued to fight, her vision slowly dimmed.

The bags of groceries shattered to the ground, her hands instinctively went to his hands, and she scratched him weakly to no avail. Her eyes rolled to the back of her head, as his dick pressed against her.

Right before she faded to black a strange thought crossed her mind- *'Damn, this nigga dick is big and harder than steel. I can't believe the last dick, I'm gonna feel belongs to the nigga that's gonna murder me.'*

***

Sa'Mage Kendricks' and two of his colleagues sat around the bar in Bennies Bar and Grill. They were celebrating the closing argument, that would seal the trial of, David 'Ice-Berg' Swanson versus the State of Texas. Tomorrow they'd make history. It was headlined across the front page of every major newspaper and magazine in the state. Tabloids made such a controversy about it, the people up high thirsted for a guilty verdict. Not only would they be taking down one of, Dallas and Fort Worth's most lucrative drug dealers. They'd also be sending a clear message to the streets. That no one was above the system. Even if they had to cheat and fabricate, they'd get you if they wanted you.

Sa'Mage was the lead District Attorney, and if tomorrow was a success his name would go straight to the desk, as the Bureau's greatest hero. He may even get the early retirement he'd been leaning towards.

"Let's make a toast gentlemen to success and justice." he smiled wickedly. "And to hefty raises," he added raising his shot glass full of, Remy Martin.

His cohorts acknowledged his offer with a drunken toast, "To success and hefty raises." As if they could care less about the justice part.

11

All three men laughed at the inside joke. Unbeknownst to either, tomorrow would end a crazy turn of events that couldn't have been anticipated, even if they had been forewarned.

Nutz sat in the stolen Caprice observing Sa'Mage's reactions. He took a deep pull of the peach flavored Phili and laughed silently, witnessing the usually well-poised attorney come unglued, as he read the text. Once Sa'Mage pulled into his driveway next to Destiny's car shit played out real funky, and he sobered up quickly.

"I wonder why she didn't pull into the garage?" He questioned unaware of his surroundings.

Sa'Mage was tipsy and horny, so he didn't notice the door to his home was ajar, or the groceries scattered all over the ground until he was up close. The scene caused him to panic instantly. His first reaction was an irrational one. He stormed the house, screaming his wife's name, hoping at any moment, she'd jump from her hiding place and tell him it was all a cruel joke.

As he paced back and forth, he turned back to the doorway. He studied the scene once more it was obvious she'd been grocery shopping. Then as if they magically appeared, he finally noticed the keys in the lock. Tears formed in his eyes as he became apparent a struggle had ensued.

"How the fuck could someone enter a gated community, and touch a District Attorney's wife?" He questioned, panic turned to fear, and he finally became coherent enough to think rationally.

He reached in his pocket for his cell, his mind was set on calling the authorities until he noticed he had three missed calls and two unread messages. He checked his messages first.

If you call the police, you will be responsible for her blood spill. In five minutes I'll let you know the bidness.

The signature at the bottom of the text read, *'The Reaper'*

Nutz smiled as Sa'Mage reread the message for the third time. "Bitch, ass nigga." He gritted as the last minute ticked into the five minutes he'd been waiting.

He grabbed his phone from the console, then speed-dialed the distraught man. After the second ring, Sa'Mage answered screaming obscenities and making threats he'd never have a chance to fulfill. Nutz listened intently, as the D.A. cried like a little bitch, and inordinately shot off questions of his Queen's whereabouts.

Tired of his ranting Nutz decided to speak. "Shut the fuck up, pussy." The silence was golden as Nutz relished in the power he held over the ever so powerful, District Attorney. His nostrils flared, as he allowed anticipation to torture the moment. "It seems as if we both hold treasures that belong to one another. I'm not an unfair man, so let's compromise," he proposed.

Sa'Mage was beside himself with confusion. He was shaking as he racked his brain in an effort to figure out how he could be so careless.

"Who the fuck are you?" he seethed. "What do you want from me? Don't you know who the fuck you're dealing with?" Sa'Mage took the phone away from his ear in fury. He placed his lips close to the mouthpiece and screamed into the phone. "Where is my wife, you, son of a bitch?" Rage sent him spiraling as tears welled in his eyes. "I don't possess anything of yours and if it's money you want, I only have four thousand in cash. Anything more you'll have to wait 'til the bank—

Before he could finish his statement Nutz lost his cool. Slapping the steering wheel, he boiled with rage. "Dig this you uptight, Uncle Tom, ass nigga." With each word, Nutz pounded a closed fist against the top of the dashboard. "I— don't— want— your— fuckin' money!" he glared at the man from the tinted windshield, Nutz couldn't stop the thought of torturing him from playing inside his head. "This shit is bigger than any amount of currency you could afford me. This shit is bigger than your career and your wife!"

Rustling could be heard from somewhere in the back of the car. As if he could see her through the back seat Nutz took a quick glimpse in the rear-view mirror, before turning his head back to Sa'Mage.

"In this life family is sacred. For mine, I'll defile every religion, go to war with God, and give my right nut." Nutz took the gun off the passenger seat and stared at it lovingly. "So, again you have something that belongs to me. More like someone, that I share air with through two different lungs. I miss my nigga, just as much as you're missing yo' bitch, right now. So, are we gonna do bidness or what?" Nutz aimed the *tool* in Sa'Mage's direction, taking mock shots.

Nutz watched as Sa'Mage racked his brain pacing on his lawn. He could tell the man loved his wife.

Sa'Mage was still confused. "I—I—I just told you. I don't have anything that belongs to your family. Do I know you? Who have I prosecuted that—" Sa'Mage stopped mid-sentence, as the epiphany hit him like a Mac truck, *'David Swanson, aka Ice-Berg! Nobody else in the state would have balls big enough, nor be treacherous enough to violate the home of a federal prosecutor.'* With tears in his eyes, the wee hours of a Monday night were tainted by Sa'Mage's laughter. The sound was so foreign it echoed through the serenity of the upscale neighborhood. He had to admit, David Swanson was an admirable man. Even from the supermax federal facility, the drug dealer was persistent.

Sa'Mage had spent the last five years trying to corner the infamous, Ice-Berg, but the crook was too slippery, always on his game. He was untouchable like Nicky Barns. Until he made the foolish mistake, of beating one of his workers half dead for trying to play him over fifteen hundred dollars on a brick he owed. This resulted in the dude yearning for revenge, siding with the F.B.I, in an attempt at bringing Ice-Berg and his team to their knees.

Now, after all his hard work and manipulation. Ice was attempting to simply walk away from being brought to justice for his bawdy ways, damn!

Noticing his demeanor change Nutz assumed the D.A.'s brain was that of a fortune teller's. "I see we are on the same page, being as though, you haven't finished your sentence." Nut awaited his response only to get none. "You don't have to speak, Counselor. Just listen, when all is said and done, we'll both get what we deserve. Tomorrow you and your office will fail to submit enough evidence. Better, yet let it be known, that the evidence you used to paint the picture of my people has been tampered with. This means all the wiretaps and fake ass witnesses you have go out the window."

Sa'Mage was furious. "So, what the fuck am I supposed to tell the Judge—my superiors?" he raged.

Nutz took the phone from his ear and stared at it as if it had offended him. Placing the phone back to his ear, he hissed his next words, "You tell them pussies to free, my mu'fuckin', nigga." He disconnected the call and tossed the phone out the window.

As he started the ignition, he heard a muffled scream. He smiled deviously, as the sound grew more consistent. Just as he was passing by the Kendricks' residence, he hit the horn and sped off. All the while, Destiny was tied at the wrists and ankles with rope, and a piece of duct tape covering her pretty lips.

Nutz slowed down to the regulated speed limit thinking, *'It would be a hell of a time to get pulled over in a stolen car, with the D.A. 's wife in the trunk.'*

Chapter Two
Business & Pleasure
Not in That Order

Snow strutted into the Fortune Five Hundred Company as if she owned the place. Her bow-legged walk demanded attention, her firm, yet round ass encouraged every investor and lawyer in the vicinity to commit visual adultery. Her blonde hair was hot combed bone straight, causing it to hang mere inches above her voluptuous ass. Her 5'9 height, said a whole lot of something.

Once she reached the receptionist, she tapped her perfectly manicured nails against the granite and marble countertop, in an imposing way. The middle-aged man behind the desk stared, becoming awestruck. He couldn't take his eyes away from her erotic look. Her sun-kissed skin, glowed under the luminous lights, causing her ocean blue eyes to exude a sense of a mystery, a sexuality.

"Excuse me, sir," she began. "I have a meeting scheduled for twelve o'clock with, Mr. Jordan, and I'm about, ummm." She glanced at her fashionable women's Rolex. "Uh, ten minutes late due to heavy traffic. You wouldn't believe the hell, I've been through, but that's neither here or there. Could you be a dear and let him know, I am truly sorry, and I'll make it up to him over brunch?"

As if he finally realized, the beautiful feline standing before him was real, he stuttered his response. Mr. um, Mr. Jordan, is currently in a meeting, but he'll be done in a few. I'll notify him of your presence, whom may I tell him you are?" He asked as he turned to the schedule book. Getting no response, he glanced back up at her.

Snow licked her lips as she replied. "Tell him, Ms. Pussy, is here to see him and I apologize again for being late."

The man was shocked. "Excuse, excuse me? Ehhh, what did you say your name is, again?" He looked as if he'd been hit with a thousand bolts of electricity.

Snow couldn't keep the smile gracing her full lips. "Ms. P-U-S-S-Y!" She spelled it out for him.

The man's face flushed. "You may take a seat." He pointed to the sitting area.

Brains sat across from Steven and Jordan's Investments. He listened intently, as Snow deceived the receptionist into believing she actually had an appointment with the multi-millionaire investor.

'So far so good', he thought as he continued listening from the microdevice, he and Snow communicated through.

His only problem with Snow's way of executing her game was that she could become so brazen with her dialect. 'Ms. Pussy'. He frowned at the notation. It was far from professional, and surely a gamble with the cards dealing with a man of, Mr. Jordan's stature.

Brains had been contriving this scheme for the last five months. He was a forty-four-year-old con, that viewed his craft as artistry. He loved the essence of deep deception and this long-awaited con was meant to be one of his most exquisite works. He was already a wealthy man, but the passion for the sport held him captive.

A slight gust of wind rustled the Wall Street Journal he was reading. He took another sip from his Starbucks cup just as a man in a tailored pinstriped, Brooks Brothers Suit sat next to him on the bench. To the public eye, the two men appeared to be merely enjoying the moment of bliss away from whatever their professions were. Yet, no one would have thought to notice, that the briefcase the man walked away with wasn't the same one he'd arrived with. The one he'd left with was filled with stacks of money for the confidential information, that only the United States Government had access to. Now it laid at the foot of a conman.

Brain smiled at Snow's success. "She's in," he said proudly.

Snow sat with her legs crossed pretending to be intrigued with her nails. Even though she noticed the well-dressed man approaching, she never took her eyes away from her cuticles.

"Excuse me, Ms.—ummm, Ms.—uhh." His uncertainty was clear.

When he was notified of his supposed meeting, his first impulse was to alert security but just as Snow forethought. The name was the only thing that intrigued him, causing him to investigate the situation.

Snow stood offering her hand. "Ms. Pussy," she clarified.

The man seemed flustered. "Okay," he began. "Well, Ms. P., can I call you, Ms. P? Pussy seems, how can I put this—vulgar."

Snow smiled at his sensitivity. "Call me whatever you like, Mr. Jordan, but pussy shouldn't be viewed as ugly or profane. At the end of the day, pussy is exactly what a real man desires. Not to mention, it's the name I was birth with, Mr. Jordan," Snow giggled at the sound of Brain's voice coming through her earpiece demanding she cut the bullshit and get to business.

Ashford Jordan stood strictly. No emotion showed on his face, but mentally he was curious of this beautiful woman's intentions. "I'm not trying to be rude, Ms. Pussy." He cleared his throat after the name, "But not only have you manipulated my receptionist, but the law. Not to mention, my time is very limited, as is my patience. So, let's cut the bullshit and give me a good reason, why I shouldn't have security escort you off the premises."

19

Snow stared into his eyes as she replied. "Security is not needed, Mr. Jordan. As we speak, I have a proposition for you, that will make you and your company millions if not billions. I merely ask for fifteen minutes of your patience. After fifteen minutes are up if you're not convinced, this is a very lucrative venture, I'll buy you dinner and pay for your wasted time."

Without a hint of amusement, Ashford Jordan turned and headed in the direction of the elevators. "Follow me, for your sake, let's hope this venture you speak of is worth my attention because if not—" He turned and gave her a devious look. "You're gonna be surprised how much my time cost, not to mention, how expensive my taste in food is."

Brains had now replaced his Wall Street Newspaper with a laptop. He typed away at the keys listening to Snow put on a beautiful performance. No woman could've played the part better. Who would have believed just eight months ago, she was a full fledge prostitute in the stable of a crazy pimp? Brains saved the man's life in a sticky situation and in return the pimp promised him a favor. He coulda never imagined, Brains had his eyes on the white beauty.

Once he proposed his request, the pimp didn't think twice about his decision. He figured that the white whore was a small price to pay when compared to what Brains had done for him. Little did he know, this particular white girl had the potential to be more than a mere prostitute. Brains had studied her mannerisms and had an epiphany. She was a gold mine and he was thinking far beyond her pussy. Now eight months later, his assumptions proved one had to be a jeweler to understand the clarity of a real diamond.

"As I was saying, Mr. Jordan, South Africa is a middle income emerging market, with an abundance of supplies to natural resources. Their stock exchange is the seventh largest in the world of modern infrastructure supporting and efficient distribution of goods to major urban centers throughout the region. Growth was robust from two-thousand four, to two-thousand eight, as South Africa reaped the benefits of macro-economic stability and global commodities.

"The only reason stability slowed down in the second half, is because of global fiscal crisis, that impacted commodities prices and demands. Yet, as we speak, the stock is rising once again in concerns of diamonds. To be exact, in two-thousand eight the exports on diamonds stood at an all-time high of eighty-one point forty-seven billion, F.O.B. Now it's twenty-seventeen and if you've been entertaining the portion of stock, you've recognized the rise in percentage." Snow paused and took a sip of water from the bottle of Ozarka, he offered her. "I have assessed two things, Mr. Jordan." From the look in his eyes, she could tell he was calculating the profits.

He stared at her intensely. "So, you are proposing, that I place my hard-earned money into a thesis built from the fibers of fact and opinion?" He asked with a raised eyebrow.

Snow smiled with assurance. "No, Mr. Jordan, I am proposing that we put our money into this thesis. I mean, isn't your whole profession built from the fibers of fact and opinion? What I am saying is your every decision is calculated risks in terms of comity, right? Listen, Mr. Jordan, I'm not here to waste your time or mine.

"I run a very successful import and export company, but the type of money it takes for me to capitalize within this venture, I don't have. You're an investor, that holds partial ownership of a fortune five-hundred company. It's in our best interest to make this move. It's profitable endeavors." Snow then did the unthinkable, she uncrossed her legs and sat with them apart, just enough so he could see, she was panty-less and freshly shaved. His eyes grew the size of golf balls at the erotic, slutty act.

"Look, Mr. Jordan, I'm willing to do almost anything for this deal to go through. If you don't trust my business sense, then please allow our lawyers to discuss the specifics over lattes and mochas."

Mr. Jordan's eyes never left her bare treasure. Perspiration began to seep through his pores, as his thoughts, lust, and desires overrode his ethical judgment. Snow observed him intently. His weakness was evident to any woman familiar with seduction. From the beginning of time, pussy has been the downfall of men. Ashford Jordan was no different from the last mu'fucka, that fell victim to its psychology.

The temperature in the spacious office seemed to rise in Fahrenheit, as Snow stood from her seat and seductively strolled around the desk. Their eyes never left each other, as she used her left hand to sweep family pictures, documents, and pens to the floor. With her right hand, she reached over and began wrapping his tie around her wrist. Pulling him closer until their lips touched.

"Solicitation is illegal, Ms. Pus—" Mr. Jordan spoke, but was cut off.

"Shhh," she hushed him. "Baby, I won't tell anyone if you don't." She softly pecked his lips, while her free hand descended towards his visible stiff shaft. "You do know that you're going overboard?"

"I should have security to remove—" Snow's tongue snaking into his mouth, cut his speech short.

His pants were undone and his small dick was now free from its confinement. Precum seeped from it, allowing Snow the pleasure of knowing she had him exactly where she wanted. While gripping his tool, she whispered the words that sealed the deal.

"Shut up, Mr. Jordan. How many other bitches have you met with a pussy this fat?" She asked releasing his manhood, sitting back on his desk.

Never taking her eyes off him, she pulled her skirt up to her waist, exposing a pair of meaty thighs, connected to her petite waist. Even though those were beautiful assets, Ashford Jordan couldn't take his eyes off her hairless pussy, pouting at him. Nectar oozed from between her lips and saturated her feminity as if she'd forgot to dry them after she'd taken a piss.

She used her middle and index fingers to spread her treasure. "Hungry?" she moaned.

Mr. Jordan loosened his tie and swallowed all in one motion. "Famished," he replied.

Brains sat back and smiled at her success. From his laptop, he sent Ashford Jordan a portfolio of everything he needed to know. Within this memo, he also sent a small attachment introducing himself, as Snow's lawyer. His smile turned into victorious laughter, as he packed up to leave.

'Snow is unpredictable,' he thought. "The plan was to fuck Jordan, but not literally. Fuck, I'm good, mami." He whispered into the device as he hailed a cab.

RENTA

Chapter Three
Assata

Lightning flashed across the Heavens as rain tainted the Earth. A strong gust of wind blew through the cemetery, causing Assata to hate his rash decision of discarding his shirt and Armani suit jacket. He stood naked from the waist up as the freezing rain seemed to make love to his skin as if it was trying to wash away his iniquities. His tears blended, with the essence of Heaven's moisture, as he whispered soft confessions into the atmosphere in hopes, of God delivering a vital message to a nigga that was dear at heart.

"Lord, I'd be lying if I told you, I've never sinned or broken a promise to you, but it was never my intentions. My 'G' from within the most untamed portions of my life, I've slain men and sold poison to my community. All in the name of shit, I considered righteous and justified, but Father—" Tears ran away from his eyes, blending with the rain. "Never have I—never have I—I—fuckkk," he screamed as anguish and venom coursed through his veins.

He stared down at the fresh soil that had been thrown on top of his right-hand man's casket. He regained his composure and continued his conversation with God. "Father never have I snatched the soul from a man, that was innocent of blasphemy." Thunder roared from deep within the sky as if God disagreed.

At that moment, the reality of never seeing or being able to fuck with his nigga again came crashing down on him. As the rain began to fall harder, it pelted his flesh. Assata crumbled to the wet grass surrounding the plot of dirt, that submerged his potna's physical being, and dug his fingers as deeply as he could into the moist earth.

"Damn, my nigga!" He moaned as if the mental pain was a physical one. "I can't believe you took this nap without me—why you leave me, dawg? I—I don't understand this type of pain, fam." Mucus drained from his nose.

Assata felt as though the rain wasn't merely soaking him externally, but somehow it found its way under his skin. It felt as if he was drowning internally, with every tear Heaven shed. "Nigga, you know, my life story. You know, how my own family left me for dead, bruh. You know the promises my, T-lady made, and how she broke them all when she died on me. You see? I can now blame you for leaving me the same way, Shy. But, why homie? Why you let them pussies kill you, my nigga? Whyyy?" Assata sobbed passionately. Unbeknownst to him, an intruder had violated his privacy.

Jazzy stood quietly, witnessing her brother's best friend lose himself in the night. Shy was her older brother, and they loved each other dearly. She'd constantly nagged him about leaving the streets, but it was a fate he'd been created for. He had a hard head, now he laid six feet beneath the same streets, he dedicated his life to. Jazzy couldn't even attend the funeral. She couldn't accept seeing her older brother, her hero in a pine box. Tears began to spill from her eyes as not only her heart but also Assata's agony killed her softly, with each word that slid from his tongue.

She'd known him her whole life. She'd craved him since she was old enough to be in tune with attraction. Assata was exactly that, a gangsta! But, he was a very loyal and respectful one. Even when she tried to seduce him with her feminist ways, he'd simply ignore her. She could recall a day when she was home alone, stepping out of the shower. She didn't even have a chance to dry off good before the doorbell rang.

Jazzy wrapped the terry cloth towel around her half-dried body and headed for the door. As she reached the living room,

Assata was already stepping through it. He was family, he'd been walking in their house for as long as she could remember. So, why he rang the doorbell was lost to her. She stood there with water dripping on the carpet and her hands on her hips in a sassy manner. For a split second, she witnessed the desire in his eyes burning dramatically, then as if the reality of who she was set in, that same lustful gaze turned into a look of disapproval.

Most guys became enchanted with her foreign features. Her cinnamon red skin complexion, her large, yet slanted grey eyes, and her short curly hair was so silky and shiny, one would think she was using chemicals. Her attributes were courtesy of her Trinidadian, mother, and father. So, to say, she was a boss bitch would be an understatement. Jazzy was loyal and kept her word, at all times. What man wouldn't die to possess a bitch, with just enough ass, nice sized titties, and fierce loyalty?

That's why seeing Assata overlooking her kinda made her feel insecure. She remembered dropping the towel allowing Assata a glimpse of her, then seventeen-year-old body. She was appalled when he rolled his eyes and walked right passed her. The next week she went off to UCLA in hot pursuit of her, Bachelor's Degree in Physiology. She'd been gone nearly three and half years.

Now, in her last semester, God seemed to have a different plan. There she stood staring at her brother's best friend, lying on top of his grave, as if the sun was out instead of the rain, that seemed to be drowning him. Jazzy figured now was the best time to make her presence known.

Assata laid on top of Shy's grave allowing the rain to beat against his skin. The wet mud covered his naked flesh, as well as stained the red Armani slacks he adorned. He gripped the twin P.90s at his sides as he stared blankly into darkness. It was as if the rain, that pelted his eyes did nothing. He felt nothing, but the cold steel in his palms. The only thing on his mind was revenge.

He suddenly began laughing at the thought playing before his eyes. "I told you, nigga—yeah—I know you was smiling down. When you saw, I showed up to your service. I stole yo' shine, nigga—hahaha. We always said we'd show up to the other's funeral one day. I did that shit, nigga." He continued laughing thinking about how the many mourners at the service stared in awe, as he stepped up to the casket choosing to be the last mu'fucka to view his dawg.

Already shirtless, fully tattooed, and his Glock nine on display. He took Shy's favorite black steel gun from his waistband, cocked it and laid it inside the casket, with a box of hollows. He then reached into his pockets and pulled out a knot of money, eighty-five thousand dollars to be exact, and tossed in there along with an ounce of Kush.

Assata saw a disturbance out of his peripheral. He gazed through his tinted Versace frames noticing Shy's moms, Leah holding a man at bay. Leah knowing her son and Assata's relationship respected the way he loved her only son. She knew if the shoe was on the other foot Shy would've done the same thing. Assata turned back to the casket, closed it on the love he'd just given, and walked out.

As he snapped back to the here and now Assata gazed down at his ruined pants, then at the white and red Gators on his feet. He sat up, laid his twins on the wet ground, and picked up the gallon of Henny, he'd brought for the occasion. Assata twisted the cap off, tilted the bottle, and allowed the Earth to have the first pleasures.

"For you, my nigga a toast to a real, nigga." He whispered, then took a long hard swallow. "Auughh," he proclaimed. The slight heat caused his face to frown up. "I should have been there, my dude—"

"Then you woulda been buried right next to him." Jazzy intervened, stepping out of the darkness.

Assata quickly tossed the bottles and snatched up his twins. He trained the infrared in the direction of her voice.

Jazzy dropped the umbrella. "It's been a long time, Assata."

The rain was no friend of people without mercy it began to soak through her Dolce and Gabbana dress. Even still, her beauty couldn't be denied. Assata stared at her through blurry eyes. He couldn't fathom this gorgeous woman being the little girl, that used to nag him with her adolescent crush and premature sense of love. He hadn't set eyes on her in three and a half years, and from this celestial image standing before him, allowing the rain to grace her skin. He could tell the journey matured her in more than a simple mental sense.

Due to the fabric of her attire being some type of silk, the rain made it seem transparent. Her dark chocolate nipples protruded against the wet fabric. It gave him a clear view of her C-cup breasts. Her 5'5 statue was thick in all the right places. The way that her hips bulged from her small waistline made it simply arduous for him to look away from her defined attributes. The ardor that consumed him carried him through a mental odyssey, that couldn't be classified as anything else, but Nirvana.

"What, I'm still too ugly to speak to?" Jazzy broke the silence.

As if her voice shook him from his state of admiration, he turned away from her and laid the twins back down onto earth. Streaks of lightning lit up the sky as he sat back down. "I'm sorry, fam," he whispered. "I should've been there for, Blood. But I—I—I—don't know what happened. I'd just gotten off the phone with, bro. Not even three hours later, I'm answering my phone to screams of y'all, ma Dukes. All she kept saying was he's gone. I didn't understand what the fuck she was talking 'bout at first, but outta nowhere, I started feeling this crazy shit, right here." He pounded on his chest. "I knew who she was talkin' 'bout, but-but—" Tears cascaded from his eyes as Jazzy shared his heart broken melody. "I shoulda been there Jazz—and maybe—maybe—"

Jazzy closed the distance between them until she was standing directly above him. Without thinking she hiked her dress up a little so that she could be comfortable in her attempt, then she sat down behind him. She pulled him close, embracing him to her bosom, wrapped her legs around his waist, and held him as he heaved and released the pain he harbored. Due to her being at his back, he couldn't see the tears spilling from her eyes like lava from a volcano.

Jazzy loved her brother deeply, as she held and rocked Assata's pain away, the rain camouflaged her tears. She made a vow, that she'd help Assata find her brother's murderers and punish them. After it was all said and done, she'd make Assata fall in love with her in the process.

**

Destiny awakened to unfamiliar surroundings, she was disoriented and cold, she couldn't remember where she was or how she'd gotten there. There was a dim light flickering on and off above her head, as she tried to move, she was stunned at the realization of her wrists tied behind her back.

"Where the hell am, I?" She questioned as panic surged through her veins.

As if needing assurance, she glanced down at her bare breasts and stared horrified at her protruding nipples. All at once the nightmare came rushing back to her. Tears cascade down her pretty face as not only the tainted visions but also the tingling sensations between her legs reminded her of her current situation.

Destiny now vaguely recalled being stripped out of her clothes, dignity, and power. She could still hear the sadistic laughter of the monster who mounted her. She could feel him as he bombarded her with his filth into her essence. She remembered hearing a door open in the distance, and as the monster was yanked off her, another horror played before her eyes. His brains were blown out of his head at point blank range.

She began weeping harder, as she recalled her hair, face, and clothes being splattered with blood and brain matter. Her heartless savior gazed deeply into her eyes and delivered his craziness.

"You need to pray that your husband is loyal to you, if not—" He absently pointed the gun at her. "It's lights out, lady." She passed out after that.

"I gotta get the hell outta here," she panicked.

Destiny attempted to sit up, but without her arms shit was useless. Suddenly, she felt a cool liquid pooling around her face, the dim light made it hard to determine where it was coming from, or what it was. As if her sense of smell kicked into overdrive, the distinctive smell of rust, filmed around her mouth. Due to her face laying against the floor it was hard to maneuver, so with all her might, she used agility to roll over onto her back.

In this position, she could see her surroundings better. I guess you can say, this small blessing was also her curse because the old cliché, *'Don't go looking for answers you can't handle.'* Became true right before her eyes.

No more than five feet away from her lied her rapist. His brains hung from his skull as puss and blood flowed like a river.

Her last thought before passing back out was, *'Please husband, please love me like you say you do.'*

***

The next morning, the courtroom was packed. Ice-Berg observed the scene, as the bailiff announced the judge.

"The State of Texas and the County of Denton, versus David Swanson, is now in session. Please stand for the Honorable Judge Carter." The bailiff announced.

Everyone stood and the short white judge entered from his chambers. The courtroom was filled with spectators. Some anticipated a guilty verdict, while others were rooting for the home team.

Intensity swallowed the atmosphere, as the judge took his seat. "Be seated," he spoke in his good ole boy drawl.

David knew he was doomed. Three counts of possession with an attempt to deliver, conspiracy to commit murder, and possession of a firearm. Not to mention, the feds still claimed to have the other shit at his head.

Mark Schutz his attorney sat poised as if he had no worries, but the actuality of the situation was that he had no faith in beating the case. He'd tried his best to get Berg to take the deal of twenty years state and thirty years feds but with them type of numbers, shid. Why not hold court? The cards were stacked against him. Schutz felt sorry for the young man because he was a good dude. He was twenty-six years old, with a whole lifetime ahead of him.

"Lord, have mercy," he whispered. He leaned over to his client's ear. "How do you feel, David?"

From the look he received he could tell, that was a stupid question.

David leaned over and replied with as much integrity as he could muster. "Dig this, Mr. Schutz, I'm a man first and a gangsta second. I knew the consequences of my actions before I sat in this chair." The two men made strong eye contact. Berg placed his hand on the older man's shoulder in a comforting gesture, "I didn't complain when I was blowin' big bread and fuckin' bad hoes in some of the most expensive suits, so there ain't no complaining now." He paused, allowing his eyes to scan the crowded room until they landed on a group of men, that looked, as though they would kill everyone in the room to ensure his freedom.

Nutz sat in the midst of the group with a look of contempt on his face. As if he could feel his brothers gaze, he turned his eyes to him. Nutz saluted him before tapping his chest with a clenched fist. Berg nodded his head in acknowledgment, then turned his attention back to his lawyer. "These hoes gave me the opportunity to save myself, but that punk shit ain't apart of the constitution I was bred under." Ice-Berg leaned back in his chair and scratched his nuts. "Fuck it, I'd rather ninety-nine years, the chair, or the needle. You did yo' job, that's all me and my locs could ask for. I'm Gucci."

"Is the State ready to proceed?" Judge Carter acknowledged the D.A.

"Yes, your Honor, the state is ready." The D.A. responded.

Judge Carter turned his eyes toward Schutz and Berg. "And you, counselor?"

"Yes, your Honor, as ready as can be."

Nutz sat on the back row in the courtroom smiling. He and his brother made eye contact. Ice-Berg had no idea of Nutz sacrifices. It was agreed there would be no communication, so he wouldn't get tied up in the sinking ship. The diamonds in his mouth glistened, as he wondered how his brother would react in the end.

"Fix yo' face, nigga—lil' bro on deck. Blood in my eyes, until you touch the ground." He whispered, then stood and walked outta the courtroom leaving behind an observer, so he'd know if the District Attorney really loved his bitch.

**

The courtroom erupted in complete pandemonium. Never in the history of the state had an attorney retracted his argument, claiming upon further investigation, that the evidence he submitted was built on lies submitted by witnesses. Who weren't credible based off their run-ins with the law. As far as the wiretaps were concerned, David 'Ice-Berg' Swanson's voice was never actually recorded.

The judge was furious. "Order in the courtroom!" he screamed. He fixed his glare on the district attorney. "So, you mean to tell me, not only are you saying this man isn't guilty of any of these heinous and unlawful crimes. But, you've also allowed this trial to continue due to a personal vendetta?"

"Uhh—uhhh, Your Honor—I—" Sa'Mage tried to explain, but his thoughts were indecipherable and crazed.

What happened next confused, as well as stunned, Judge Carter. Sa'Mage Kendricks' crumbled to the floor and cried like a child. Nevertheless, the verdict was in.

"Has the jury reached a verdict?" A balding Hispanic man stood for the judge.

"Yes, your Honor—we the jury finds the defendant, David Swanson not guilty of all charges he has been accused of." The juror states.

The courtroom erupted once again. Ice-Berg and his lawyer sat speechless. Never in a million years did they expect this outcome. Ice-Berg turned in his seat just in time to see his little brother Nutz making his exit, right before he turned, and locked eyes with him. The small wink he gave let Ice-Berg know everything he needed to know. *Real niggas do real things!*

***

Destiny awakened for the second time. This time she was well aware of her predicament. Even though she was still a little boggled, her instincts told her she was not alone. Suddenly, a tall figure stepped from the shadows. Destiny's breath caught, as the intruder descended upon her. He was dressed in all black attire, complimented by a black ski mask, hiding his facial features, he squatted down and sat her upright. Now eye to eye, the man's eyes became beautiful to her.

For some strange reason, she lost herself in the turquoise pupils, as she did her breath quickened. Anger flooded her veins, as she questioned herself, asking how she could allow herself to lust after a man she hadn't even seen? Thirst for a man, that was possibly going to take her life?

"Listen," he began. "This was all bidness, love. What this sucka did to you—" he nodded his head at the corpse. "Was never part of my plans. Your husband just chose the wrong profession." He then allowed his eyes to travel the length of her slender frame.

Destiny feared he'd have predatorial thoughts, so she spoke the first words that came to mind. "Please, don't rape me again, just kill me." Tears escaped her eyes all over again.

The masked man laughed. "Rape you? Look, lady— wrong, nigga. I just told you, I'm not with that shit. Why do you think, ole boy's brains are all over the place?" He smiled as if he'd done something romantic.

Destiny was beyond angry at this point. "What the fuck do you find funny?"

The masked man smiled. "You."

She couldn't believe his audacity. As she decided to give him the lashing of his life, her eyes were drawn to the gigantic .357 he gripped with his gloved hand.

"Why don't you just let me go?" she whispered. Looking into his eyes she trembled at what had his attention. He stared, lustfully at her pussy. "Please, let—me—gooo—" she cried.

In one swift motion, the man stood to his feet and placed his pistol in his waistband. He bent slightly over and placed his arms under her armpits, lifting her to her feet, effortlessly.

"Turn around—" he demanded.

Fear consumed her, as she thought of a million excuses to give him, in order to stop him from doing whatever it was he had planned. "No, please don't," she pleaded.

The man seemed impatient and tired. He spun her around quickly. All the while, she screamed, trying to resist, but the rope binding her ankles and wrists only tightened.

"Shut the fuck up, woman, and be still! Please." Something inside his voice stilled her.

Suddenly, the ropes binding her wrists was cut loose. Surprise surged through her, as her mind tried to wrap around what was happening.

The man turned her facing him, so that they were eye to eye, without turning his gaze from hers. He squatted, then sliced through the rope restraining her ankles. He raised his head just enough to be eye level with her crotch. Gazing up at her, he planted a soft kiss on her kitty.

"Get dressed, Ms. Lady." He pointed to her neatly folded clothes, resting on a wooden crate in the far corner of the room.

"What's going on?" She asked in disbelief.

The masked man stood to his feet and replied. "I'm taking you home."

***

Sa'Mage was distraught as he waited for the phone call. All sorts of thoughts surged through his mind. Him being disbarred from his practice. What every station and paper in the nation would say about him in the morning? His colleague's opinions of him? Despite, all that nothing mattered more to him at this point, but the return of his wife.

"How did I get her into this craziness?" he wondered.

He could practically hear her as if she was standing there in his presence.

"Your job is gonna be the death of us." She'd screamed during one of their many arguments.

This one caused by anonymous phone threats received due to a high-profile case he was prosecuting. The vibrating of his BlackBerry startled him from his memory.

"Hello?" He answered without the slightest glimpse of the display screen.

He could hear her whimpering and incomprehensible gibberish. Chills ran down his spine as recognition flooded his spirit. "Destiny, baby, where are you?"

"I can't—do—this—anymore, I'm—I'm so—" The crying became hysterical.

He heard the phone crash to what he assumed to be the floor. "Destiny, baby, where are you? Let me know so that—"

"Hello?" A voice interrupted his pleading.

"Baby, I'm so, so sorry that—"

"Hello?" The feminine voice interrupted once again.

Something conversant about this voice brought tears to his eyes as recognition set in. The voice belonged to Destiny's mother. The same mother who talked her husband into loosening his grip on his baby girl's life.

"Sa'Mage?" she hissed. "How fucking dare, you allow this to happen to my youngest daughter? Sa'Mage—you're a poor excuse of a husband. Even if it takes my last breath, I will keep you away from my child. You better pray, my husband has a good heart because you have disgraced this household, as well as your own. Don't try to contact Destiny ever again!"

"But, Mrs. Black, I—I—" That's when he was introduced to the dial tone.

***

Ice-Berg stared at his younger brother admirably. He was at lost for words as Nutz told him the lengths he went through to recapture his freedom. Nutz acted nonchalant about the whole episode. To him, loyalty was everything his loyalty to his big brother, held no limitations.

"So, now what? What's the business from here on out? You know, that shit is gonna be turned all the way up, right? These crackers don't like to see a nigga outsmart them. They're gonna be aimin' at your shower cap now," Nutz questioned.

Ice-Berg nodded his head in agreement, as his life flashed before his eyes. "Dig, lil' bro. You gave me breath again. I can't repay you for that, a nigga was done for."

Nutz watched something dark enter his brother's eyes. Something like dark clouds seemed held in place by misplaced pride. Ice-Berg stood and glanced around the high-rise apartments. The plush white carpet felt thicker, the black and white décor, and marble finishing appeared more detailed.

'When a man is shown, his life can be taken away in the blink of an eye. He learns to appreciate the small shit.'

Walking over to the large picture window he stared out at the rain slick street. "Bro— so, the least I can do is keep it one hundred with you, just like I always have. Bro, I'm right back at 'em. Not only am I gonna flood the city worse than before. But, while I am doing it, I'm going to murder every one of them suckas who took the stand against me." Ice-Berg vowed.

RENTA

Chapter Four
A Beautiful Con

The owner of the Black Dodge Magnum stepped out of his house with a smile on his face. To the naked eye, he would pass as a Boss Nigga. True enough his grind allowed him the pleasures of splurging on his lavish lifestyle. Not only did he own a two-story, five-bedroom home, that was fully furnished with imported furnishings. He also owned a Lambo Diablo, a 'G' Wagon, two Jags, and the Black Mag that sat on 26s parked in front of his house at the moment.

To say that he was on money would be an understatement. To the average ears, the nigga would probably be considered, the realest nigga alive if judged by his cover. Yet, a book should never be judged by its cover, because when writing his own book, the fakest nigga can become one of the realest. This man was a prime example of the cliché, *'there's no loyalty amongst thieves'*.

Just two weeks ago, he was summoned to pay his debt to the federal government. For his cooperation testifying against his then best friend, Ice-Berg. He received a pardon from his offenses of Interstate Trafficking attempting to distribute fifteen bricks of pure Columbian Coke and tax evasion. But to him, as well as, the Government's horror, Berg somehow slid through the crevices. No one knew how he did it except the ones that needed to know.

His written confession would have hung, Berg being as though he was his everyday accomplice. To make matters worse, he had convinced his girl, Tisha Swanson. The love they shared superseded the devotion she had for her own brother. It's no secret that dick can blindfold a woman to some of the purest shit. Tisha was as weak for a fat dick and good game as they come. It killed Berg knowing his baby girl turned on him for a sucka, but God worked in dangerous ways. Because revenge was a fine cuisine and Berg planned on partaking of its pleasures.

The magnum idled at the curb as a woman stood beside it awaiting his presence. She was the temporary replacement, that his designated driver Big Moon appointed him. Being that he trusted Big Moon's judgment he never even gazed at the woman until this moment. Now that she stood before him, he could at least say Moon had great taste. Even though she wasn't his usual type, Lil' Mama was sexy as she wanted to be. She stood about 4'9 and weighed about one-hundred, twenty pounds. Her dreads hung low in a very erotic design. Although she was small she was well compacted, from her posture one could tell she knew she was bad.

"Good day, Mon." She spoke in a sultry Jamaican accent.

The informant strolled over to where she stood and towered over her with an intense gaze. "What's a beautiful woman like you doing drivin' mu'fuckas around instead of mu'fuckas drivin' you around?" he critiqued.

Lil' Mama instantly peeped his game and replied. "Money waits fa no man. Meh, maybe beautiful to he but dat don't mean meh don't have to work to earn my keep just like everyone else, star. Now if you want to you can drive me around and show me de city," she smiled seductively.

The man smiled. "Naw, mami, I'm good on that, but you dine with a boss later tonight, kool?"

She slyly moistened her lips. "Aye, mon tats cool." She then opened his door and waited for him to slide in the backseat.

As she made her way to the driver's side something caught her eye. A sky-blue CTS sat on the opposite side of the street, three car lengths away. The car itself wasn't what intrigued her. It was the silhouette of the driver, that captured her attention. He sat real low in his seat trying to be inconspicuous, but the soft glow from whatever he was smoking gave him away. As she slid behind the wheel, she took one last glance at the vehicle before pulling off.

'Damn—me, buggin',' she thought as she pulled outta the subdivision.

She glanced back at the man of the hour and asked if she could put on some music, he nodded and continued his phone conversation.

***

Ice-Berg allowed a solitary tear to fall from his right eye, as he stood over his baby sister with a silencer-equipped pistol planted directly between her eyes. She cried sincerely, as she stared into the eyes of her bloodline. What she saw was the essence of disdain, hurt, and anguish.

"I'm sorry, Berg—I con—co—confused," she sniffled. "I was so—"

"Shhh," Ice-Berg, shushed her. "It's Gucci, sis. I know what love and loyalty will do to a mu'fucka."

Tisha's face relaxed into a sense of hope. "Yeah, I know right. I mean this some crazy shit. I feel so bad, kuz you always told me, that loyalty was to death. I violated the motto. Betrayal is suicide—I know, I fucked up, Berg. I'll never cross you again. I mean—you just said, you understand how love and loyalty can fuck a person up. I mean—how would mama have reacted if you killed me? Boy, untie me from this chair and let's wait on, Butta, to come back home. He's not family anyway. You love me, right?"

Tears fell from both their eyes as he replied. "Yeah, I understand, that even family will betray you for their own reasons." He then squeezed the trigger at point blank range. Tisha's body crumbled over. "Yeah, I understood, sis—"

***

Teasley Lane the Jamaican woman stopped at a red light and noticed the same sky-blue CTS from earlier creeping up behind them.

"Ahhh, aayyyee, mon—member the Blue CTS me told chu of bock at tee house?" she questioned.

"Yeah, what 'bout it?" he asked curiously.

"Well, mon, tere it is again."

The man turned his head in the direction she pointed, and as if life took on a slow-motion scene Nutz pulled up just enough, that they were almost eye to eye. He was grinning like the devil.

"Go," he screamed. "Drive this mu'fucka, now!"

But to his utter confusion, the car didn't move. He turned back to the woman, to find out why the fuck she wasn't following orders only to find a .44 mag pointed at his face. He tried to react, but he was a little too late. A slug penetrated his face and he died with his eyes open.

"Berg say to tell chu tanks fa being a good friend." She spit on his limp body and climbed out the car.

In broad daylight, she grabbed the gas can Nutz held out of the window to her and drenched the inside of the magnum, then set it aflame. Without remorse, she slid into the passenger side of the CTS, smiling at her handy work.

Nutz pulled into traffic slowly once the light changed for the 3rd time. A grey Ford Explorer was parked two blocks away awaiting their arrival. The CTS would suffer the same fate as the man and the black mag they'd left blazing.

***

Her sweat dripped onto his face as he raised her leg high in the air. She was positioned on her side smiling back at him mischievously.

"Do it, mutherfucker," she taunted.

Feeling his manhood being tested, he used his dick to massage the length of her pussy lips.

Snow enjoyed his foreplay so much, she began rubbing her clit. "Uummm," she purred as he slid into her essence.

He stroked her long and deep as their tongues danced. All in a moments time and without her consent or preparation, he slid outta her kitty and positioned the head at her backdoor. Slowly he worked the head into her forbidden treasure. Hastily, she tried to get her leg down, but his grip was firm, and he inched his muscle deeper into her.

"Shiiit—it—it hurts you, muther—fucker! T—take—take it out," she protested.

As he submerged his thick seven inches in her ass, he whispered, "Just relax, love—I promise you'll enjoy it soon enuff." All the while his stroke became more intense.

"Oohhh shit. Babyyy—shisss," she cried.

She began playing with her clit as fast as she could, trying to turn the pain into pleasure. He noticed this and began pumping faster. Snow's pleasure was suddenly over the edge, she began working her hips as her ass got wet.

"Tell me, I'm your dirty, white whore. Tell me, those black bitches can't fuck you like I do. Tell me, mutherfucker—" she screamed taking his dick in her ass like a porn star.

"Oh shit, take this black dick bitch," he growled as he began to feel the sensations that came with an explosive nut.

His back stiffened, as he tried to control the eruption, yet just as he began to tame the beast raging through him.

Snow began experiencing a strange development and lost it. "Oh—my—fuckin'—Jesus," she screamed.

The tightened of her ass cheeks made the man release into her essence.

Brains relaxed in the lobby of the Hilton. He listened intently as Snow gave herself to a man she'd been seducing for the past three weeks. This escapade would be the key to their success. The man in question was none other than, Ashford Jordan's Representative and Legal Advisor.

Brains couldn't contain the feelings surging through him. It was like Snow's success gave him a hard-on, and something to be proud of, all at once. He smiled standing to leave. "Good girl—fuckin' good girl—"

***

Four hours later

Antone's Barbershop was empty except for three occupants. They engaged in a conversation, that could and would get each of them a conspiracy case if this particular dialogue ever left this room.

"Dig, Tone, I've known you since you were a pup, right? I've taken you in and been as close to a father figure than you've ever had, right?"

Tone nodded in silent agreement leaning back in his chair. "Now, look, Bobby Ray." He addressed Brains by his government. "Don't walk into my establishment insulting me, old man. You know you can miss me wit' the spill and tell ole Tone what you need, and it's done. I owe you my life and even after that, I'll be in debt to you for introducing me to the feel of alligator shoes. So, spit it out. What can I do for you, old head?"

Brains smiled, "Look, I'm embarking on a new venture, I'm playin' on. I'm not tryin' to run a cap. I got a sucka in my web. I'm not tryin' to let 'em loose, till I suck 'em clear of his hard-earned grip. This one kinda risky, yet the takeoff is a masterpiece." Snow laughed at his excitement.

Brains was so amped his hand gestures were borderline comical. Shooting up from his seat, he began pacing the floor and continued explaining his plans. "It's going to take every piece on the board to fleece this mark and get to the other side of the board to capture the king." Suddenly he spun and locked eyes with, Tone. "Now, in order to capture this king, we must be overly strategic and precise with our advance."

Tone nodded his head in understanding as Brains started pacing again. There was a studious look on his face, as he slammed a closed fist into the palm of his hand.

"The king's financial status was the strength behind his empire, but understand even though, the mighty dollar is the element that keeps the world spinning. It all boiled down to a mu'fucka, that's controlling it and the heart that he possesses to keep it." He paused midstride and trained his eyes on Snow. "This king we're seeking to hoodwink his heart is too meek." Brains slowly stalked over her like a hungry panther, with an eye contact only they could understand. Brains turned his eyes to Tone his empire was crafted off pure genius. Yet, he lacked the spine to hold onto the power he had incurred. Everything was set, except one final, but vital detail."

Tone raised his brow in inquisition. Brains facial expression was serious.

He waved a manicured hand around the conservatively decorated room. "We need to turn this barbershop into imports and exports distribution." Tone shrugged his shoulders. "A man of your prestige shouldn't have a problem with that small detail."

Brains glanced at his Swiss Watch then allowed his gaze to settle on, Snow. She took this as her cue to deliver the final blow to seal the con.

"The problem doesn't lie within the ability to create the illusion," she said.

Tone looked baffled. "So, where does the problem lie?" Snow smiled seductively, as she glanced at her Rolex. "The problem lies in time. We have precisely two hours and twenty-nine minutes to cover ground and convert this place into a relatively respectable place of business. But first, you need to terminate all your hair appointments and inform your employees, that they have the day off with pay. We have a team on standby. Plus, it would be a complete catastrophe if we're in the middle of the biggest pay off of our lives and a line of nappy headed mutherfuckers storms in for their usual taper fade."

The room exploded with laughter. Brains pulled out his iPhone and held the #1 down for his associates he had on speed dial. Whoever answered the other end listened, as Brains spoke briefly. He merely said, "Bring in the equipment."

Snow couldn't prevent the sensations shooting through her body. Money simply made her pussy wet. "Showtime," she whispered.

***

Detective Hunter scribbled in his notepad, as the ghettofied woman recalculated her version of the brutal murder committed six hours ago. "So, you say, two men and a woman pulled up in a blue vehicle. The woman jumped out of the passenger side and opened fire on the deceased?"

The woman rolled her eyes and smacked her lips. "Look, Mr. if you're really trying to catch who did this, you need to get the story correct. Ain't nobody said the woman opened fire. I said the bitch's hair was fire. She had these dreads that was oh so cute and—"

Detective Hunter put his hand up. "Ma'am—I'm not interested in the woman's head. We're trying to solve a murder here." He turned to the crowd. "Did anybody see what happened here today?"

A girl with purple and black hair stood defiantly and replied. "Ain't no snitches out here cracker."

Fed up, Detective Hunter turned and walked away. He snickered at the obscenities that landed on his back. Forensics combed the area, as numerous law enforcement analyzed, and congregated around the crime scene. Due to the fact, the victim had ties with the Bureau the boys up high was definitely on deck.

"Hey, Hunter, wait up." A feminine voice deviated him from his destination.

She stood at least five feet tall and had shoulder length hair, that was always pulled back into a tight ponytail. Her skin wasn't flawless, but it wasn't overly blemished either. She resembled a lady basketball player with a homely face.

"How are you, Detective Winslet?" Hunter stopped allowing her to catch up.

"I could be better if dead bodies weren't popping up all over the city."

Hunter raised his brow. "Bodies as in more than one?"

Winslet looked at him through questioning eyes. "What, you mean to tell me, you weren't notified about the murder of twenty-year-old, Tisha Swanson?"

Detective Hunter stood emotionlessly. Even though his mental was racing full speed. *'Ice-Berg's younger sister?'* he thought.

Being an investigator on the Swanson case had caused him many sleepless nights and massive heat on the home front. He vividly, remembered the hurt and animosity, that burned in Ice-Berg's eyes when he was told his sister and best friend was willing to testify against him.

"Hunter—Hunter, are you alright?" Winslet brought him out of his reverie.

"Huh? Yeah—yeah—I was just wondering how, Mr. Swanson, is going to react to the news of his baby sister and best friend losing their lives on the same day?"

Winslet knew how hard Hunter worked to bury David 'Ice-Berg' Swanson under the confines of a federal max prison. Only to watch with astonishment the hard work and late nights shattered in vain.

"Well—she began—I pray, the Lord has mercy on me for what I am about to say, but it's the truth. I hope that the deaths of his family bring him to his knees and shows him the grief he's caused all of us and many others." She glanced over at the taped off area surrounding the charred Dodge Magnum. There was no need for the ambulance, the coroner was wide-eyed, as they closed the doors on the burnt corpse.

Hunter smiled. The chase was back on, but this time, Berg was going down and staying down. "Naw, Detective, I don't think this shit-head mutherfucker will be grieving too much over these two. In fact, I think, he's more informed about the deceased than we are."

Detective Winslet stared at him perplexed. "What would make you say that, Hunter?"

Hunter smiled. "Oh—it's just a hunch. Let's go over to Catrina's Deli over on Hickory and talk about it over a cup of her Trinidadian Joe."

***

The sleek, black, stretch limo pulled in front of 'World Commodities.' Ashford Jordan and his legal advisor, Justin Crow sat behind the tinted windows enjoying the sounds of soft classical music. Jordan sipped from a chilled glass the amber color Brandy seemed to hypnotize him, as he stared at its substance like he could actually see the actual ingredients. He pretended to be listening to the counselor, as he bitched about the corruption of wall street, but Ashford had his mind on the erotic escapade Snow had taken him on.

He stirred the two ice cubes that chilled his cognac. His thoughts carried him away and the deeper he traveled, the more blood rushed into his male organ. A devilish smile crept across his face as he reflected on how Mrs. Waynebrook. Who Snow properly introduced herself as after they copulated did things to him he'd seldom fantasized about.

Justin Crow felt disrespected. "Mr. Jordan—Mr. Jordan? Do you hear me? These assholes are trying to ruin the stock market. Bryant and Westbrook Internationals are buying up this new clinical drug and—" he stopped midsentence and stared in bewilderment. "What's so, funny? What's the cheesy smile for, Mr. Jordan?"

Distracted from his trip down memory lane Ashford decided to give his prick of an attorney his attention. "Since, you must know, Justin. I was just thinking about this wonderful woman we are about to invest our hard-earned money into. She's beautiful."

Justin couldn't help but smile. "Not to mention, very—very creative." He responded allowing his own thoughts of Snow to overpower his mental. He vividly recalled how tight she felt as he fucked her in the ass.

"Creative?" Ashford asked realizing his slip-up.

Justin refocused his eyes on his client, only to find him staring quizzically. "Business. She's very creative and business savvy!"

Chapter Five
'Bidness Savvy'

"Sell now the share is losing interest!" Snow screamed at the flat screen showing apparent decreases in sales.

Ashford Jordan watched in amazement as she shouted orders at thirty investors set up in the vast opening. He stared up at the screen mounted on the far wall to his right. The digital showed the share in platinum was declining considerably. A glance at the action going on in the room was intense as the consumer market unfolded before him. As he studied his surroundings a slight smile crept across his lips.

Standing next to him was his lawyer and next to Justin stood Tabius Malone, Ms. Waynebrook's lawyer. In order to be heard over the ruckus, he leaned over and verbalized his excitement.

"This may be one of the best investments we've ever made."

Justin simply nodded his agreement, as he fantasized about the many ways, he planned to lavish himself with his newfound wealth, he and Snow planned on embezzling from his employer. After the check was signed the plan was to have the currency transferred to an offshore account, then simultaneously, Ashford would meet his demise by way of a terrible accident. Even better there would be no evidence implicating him to the crime.

He and Snow would be free to enjoy their quest on the beautiful island of the West Indies. The group of islands divided between the British and U.S. serving as a landmark constituting their territory, the Virgin Islands to be exact. A perfect place for one or two to retire.

"Justin!" The sound of his boss's voice raided his reverie.

"Huh? Oh, my apologies, Mr. Ashford. I was simply thinking about what the USA Today said about the market."

Ashford Jordan's eyes studied him intently. "Oh really, and what might that be? It had to be something intriguing, that you couldn't hear your name being called—three times to be exact."

Justin stared back at him uneasy and replied. "It basically spoke on how shifty the market could be at times but due to this new tracking device system called Sigfig—"

Jordan cut him off abruptly. "What does Sigfig have to do with your—"

"If you'll let me finish, I'll explain," Justin countered.

Ashford smiled a wry smile and motioned for him to continue.

"As I was saying Sigfig keeps track of your investments. The investment service keeps track of your average per day up to a sixth-month average. Their largest holdings, most bought and most sold. More than a million investors nationwide, with total assets of forty-five billion, managed their investment portfolios online with Sigfig."

Ashford didn't understand why this bit of information should mean anything to him, or his lawyer being as though, they were about to invest not one, not two, but three million dollars of his hard-earned money into the world commodities. Little did he know, Justin was beginning to get cold feet about the treachery, lurking in the darkness. Yes, Snow was a beautiful, smart woman, with an amazing sex drive. But, was she worth life in prison? A sickening feeling overcame him, as he visualized himself going to prison for capital murder. It would ruin him.

Not to mention, he wasn't cut out for a prison cell. He'd be somebodies bitch before the second day. Fuck the islands this scandal, he wanted no parts of. So, in an attempt to plant the seed a better way, as well as a safer way to invest his money, he threw Sigfig out there on a limb.

"I too have done my research on the tracking device Sigfig," Malone spoke for the first time. "But, you must understand, that whatever company you choose to invest in there's always the possibility of markets switching directions." Malone smoothed his hand over his Brooks Brothers suit, brushing away invisible lint.

Anyone who knew him knew the twitching of his left eye was a clear indication of his fury. He turned his attention to Ashford in an attempt at discrediting Justin's word.

"A particular share maybe on the rise this week showing no sense in change, but the next moment, you check interest, you find that particular market has crashed. No device can rationalize better than the human brain, so why even consider it?" Malone turned facing the action in the room. He emphasized his point with a sweeping hand gesture. The room was buzzed with activity. "The stock market is rise and fall, risks and rewards, but I can assure you, World Commodities is as stable as they come and has the potential to multiply, even triple your investments into a larger fortune."

After he assured, as well as canceled, Justin's attempts he turned his attention to the insidious lawyer. "Mr. Crow, may I have a word with you in regard to the paperwork needed to finalize our dealings?" He proposed with a deceiving grin.

"Ummm—I—I think that—"

Before he could finish, Ashford Jordan patted him on his back with a bit of order. "That sounds wonderful. I'll be here when you get back."

Just as he was about to decline, Snow appeared from the midst of ringing phones and excitement in the room.

"Now that you and your lawyer have witnessed my business etiquette can we get back to the matter at hand?" Her aura was lascivious as she stared into Mr. Jordan's eyes. Turning her gaze to the two lawyers she could sense the tension staining the air.

"Is there a problem, Malone?" She addressed her lawyer.

With an evil glare, he replied. "No, not at all. Me and my fellow colleague are about to go over a couple details, we'll return shortly. Why don't you keep Mr. Jordan occupied until we do?" Malone replied.

From the look in his eyes, she could tell something was off. She nodded in accordance. Without taking her eyes away from, Justin Crow she thought, *'Damn, he had some good dick! Such a waste, such a fuckin' waste.'*

***

~3 Months Later~

Since his release, Ice-Berg crashed the asphalt with an iron fist. Due to the exposure of his case his old connect politely cut him off, but a good connect was nothin' to a boss. Instead of crying over spilled milk, he painted the city red with the blood of the transgressors who violated him in the worse way. Yet, any real nigga, that's ever dealt with men who were connected knew getting money and bloodshed never coexisted.

As he bled his enemies his mind never strayed from the mission of securing a good connect. Which is how at this moment, he found himself at a roundtable, positioned by an Olympic sized swimming pool. He stared out at the silhouette of a naked, feminine, deity swanning below the surface of the clear waters. The tables were decorated with fresh fruits, blueberry pancakes, an assortment of juices, sausages, and coffee. The mini mansion standing behind him blew his mind.

It was designed with Greece in mind even out in the massive yard, statues of Greek Gods, were sporadically stationed. The whole experience made him realize, he was merely an accomplished hustler. He would have to step up his game to live the life his new connect Russia was living. The sound of splashing water stole his attention from the beauty of his surroundings, only to have it stolen again by a much more magnificent sight.

The bronze Goddess emerged from the pool with an elegance that was almost risqué. She had perfect sized breasts, a hairless pussy, and a small waist complimenting her curvy, yet petite frame. As she dried her hair with the towel, that was just minutes ago folded neatly at the edge of the pool, their eyes met. At first, she seemed slightly startled, but as she continued to study his poised nature and boss etiquette. Her dark, hypnotic eyes filled with raw, animalistic, lust swan within her essence.

At that moment, Ice-Berg realized this gorgeous feline standing before him was extremely insidious. He could tell that behind the beautiful eye and radiant smile, she now blinded him with was something dark. She seductively slid her bikini bottoms over her curves, allowing him a few more delicious seconds at viewing her feminist treasure. Finally done with her teasing, she draped the towel over her slender shoulders and erotically walked in his direction.

As she descended upon him her nipples jutted out towards him. They were the size of silver dollars and the same hue of her luxurious hair, that was slicked back, hanging past her plump ass cheeks. Now standing within his orbit she seemed even more breathtaking. She reached over and grabbed a strawberry from the selection of fruits without acknowledging him.

Ice-Berg wondered who she was, yet didn't want to be disrespectful. He turned his attention back to the lawn and its brilliance.

"Even though thu exterior appears to be calm, me can almost bet, thu dick is hard and your curiosity is getting the best of thu." Yet, thu're too respectful to speak on thu desires, or thu fear me husband so mush, that a look is the only attention that thu'll afford me." Her Ecuadorian accent was thick. "Thu silly Amadacans and thu silly ways," she giggled.

Finally turning his eyes back to her, he laughed inwardly, yet his façade never changed. The hilarious part was that she was absolute. His dick was hard as granite for sure and he was too respectful to do anything other than look, but even that was considered a sin, now that he knew what the gigantic diamond ring bulging from her finger represented.

"Umm, I think you forgot the top of your bikini by the pool," he began.

First silence, then gentle laughter. Ice-Berg glanced down at his diamond-encrusted Rolex. "I don't mean to sound impatient, but do you know what's taking your husband so long?"

The beauty simply rolled her eyes before answering. "Me, husband, believes the world operates on his time. He is probably out on the green acting like he's the Russian version of Tiger Woods. But, if he's scheduled a meeting with thu, he'll be here soon."

Belle pulled out a chair across from him and took a seat. "Now—" with an open hand she introduced herself. "My name's, Belle. The wife of the great man thu are about to see."

Ice-Berg studied her feminisms for a few seconds. It was beyond him how the woman felt so comfortable, sitting topless, at the table with a stranger and still extrude the aura of a respectable woman.

He released the first words that came to mind. "Aphrodite."

She gazed at him inquisitively. "Aphr—ite? I no understand tis word. Tell me more about this Aphro? Umm—aphr." She used her hands to express her nonunderstanding.

Ice couldn't stop laughing. She stared at him with a puzzled look. "What's so damn funny?"

This only made him laugh harder. "I'm very sorry, love— I'm sorry." He slowly regained his composure. "Aphrodite— she was a Greek Goddess of love and beauty." He allowed his eyes to reveal his meaning.

A small smile crept across her pouty lips. "Are ju trying to say, that thu find me to be beautiful?"

Fire danced in his eyes as he ventured out onto the edge of his conversation. "No, sweetheart, I'm saying you are beautiful. Not *trying* to say, and as for the comment you made earlier, about me being too respectful or simply fearful of your husband? Belle, I'm a gangsta in my own right. Respect, your husband has earned his place at the table, so of course, I regard him with a certain amount of revere. But, fear, he bleeds like every other nigga, I've met.

"I don't know how they rock in Rome, but I'm from the grit of the lone star state fear becomes a deadly element when associated with mu'fuckas that ain't got it together. This lifestyle this gonna be me one day. This game wasn't created with fear in mind. Only bosses are allowed at the long table. I'm the definition of a boss's etiquette. So, with all due respect, pop your eyes out of their sockets, place them on your tongue, and watch what you say to me."

Belle reached over and grabbed another strawberry from the platter and gently placed the tip of it between her lips. Without taking her eyes away from his she partook of it.

Sensually, placing the half-eaten fruit back on the platter, her eyes seemed to darken as she studied him. "Your balls must be very big Mr—Umm, thu never gave me, thu name."

Standing to make his departure, he directed his attention to a huge statue of the Greek God, Apollo to his left. "Tell your husband, I find it very disrespectful, that he conducts business this way. Good day, Mrs. Belle." Turning to leave he walked straight into a hulking figure.

The first man, he'd just ran into, stood at least six-five, and weighed over two-hundred sixty pounds. He was dressed in all black, with a visible Bluetooth in his ear, and black Ray Ban sunglasses adorned his muscular face, hiding his glare. The second man, to his right, was in identical attire but wasn't as menacing. They had their hands in their suit jackets, undoubtfully grasping instruments that caused death.

"Butch—Gruco, settle down fellas." A baritone voice sounded from behind the pair.

At his request, the two men relaxed their hands and stepped to the side. His appearance was contradicting when you compared it to his profession. He stood about five-ten at best. He had deep-set blue eyes, that shocked you at first glance. The scar that ran from the middle of his eyebrow to the middle of his cheek, was what gave him up as a man, that had dirty dealings. His sandy blonde hair was long and curly. Outside of these few attributes, one would never peg him for a Russian drug Caesar.

Yet, he was one of the most dangerous men on this side of the hemisphere.

A crooked grin graced his lips as he extended his hand— "Mr. Swanson, pleasure to meet you."

Taking his hand in a firm grip Ice-Berg returned the grin. "Berg will be just fine, Swanson sounds so formal, don't you think?"

"Berg, you say? As in, 'Ice-Berg', the infamous king pen, that the whole state is pissed at for finding a way to piss on the Judicial System? Ice-Berg, the twenty-six-year-old, David Swanson, that lives in a four bedroom, two and half bath, red brick home, located on the outskirts of Denton, Texas, in a small town named, Argyle? The ballsy young man, that possesses a quick trigger finger and a lust for exotic women? Berg, of course." After revealing to Ice-Berg that he'd done his homework, he turned his gaze to his beautiful wife, who was now applying suntan lotion on her perky breasts

"Speaking of exotic women—Belle, excuse yourself, my dear wife. You have no place amongst men."

She gathered her things and made her exit, but before she could pass Russia called to her. "Wife stand before me."

Belle stopped between the four men and stood before him. Palming her naked breasts he began massaging the left one. "Exotic wouldn't you say, my friend, Berg? A diamond from the North-Western coast of South America. Ecuador, to be exact." Now pinching her hardened nipples his eyes burned into hers. The pain he was causing her wasn't evident to the masses, yet the two of them understood its implications. Yet and still, she seemed inured to his actions.

"Ecuador has an abundance of beautiful things, but please understand my friend, beauty is merely the death of a foolish man. The splendor of our visionary has been our downfall from the beginning of time. Once one obtains beauty, he also obtains a million enemies for everybody desires the beautiful, never knowing that kingdoms has fallen, men have been betrayed, and deaths have followed in its wake. All for the sake of beauty." With that being said, he kissed her forehead and dismissed her. Then with cold eyes, he turned his sights back to, Ice-Berg. "Now—let's talk business."

***

As Ashford Jordan typed away at the computer keys a funny feeling invaded his senses.

"Maybe we need to wait for our lawyers return." Him and Snow were now in the confines of her office, which was actually Antone's, but Jordan was none the wiser.

The events that led him to the laptop Snow provided for him was stimulating, as well as deceptive, depending on whose viewpoint one was looking from. It all began once the door to the office closed and secrecy enclosed their dealings. Snow seduced him right out of his trousers. In seconds, she had his dick deep down her throat and his balls clenched lightly.

"Oh, my God," he moaned as she rapidly bobbed up and down on his member. His hands became lost in the blonde locks as he gripped her head and fucked her mouth. "Shiii—shittt—my fucking wife—ohhh! She—she's going to divorce—uhhh, shittt."

Snow stared up at him and studied his expression. The pleasure, that radiated from his face, and the pulsating of his penis confirmed her suspicions, he was about to cum.

"I'm abo—bout to—umm, to cum. Keep going, baby suck it! Suck this dick!" Ecstasy cried from his lips.

In order to bring her plans to fruition, she slowly slid away from his erect muscle. Yet, he still tried to chase his moment of bliss. She literally had to pry his hands away from her head.

"What's the problem?" he wondered.

Seizing the opportunity Snow stood and straightened her attire. "I have a glorious idea." She replied as she walked around her desk and opened the Dell laptop computer that rested on top of it.

She began typing until she accessed what she was looking for. "You do know how to access your own account, don't you? Or does Justin spoon feed you with your own money?"

Pride was a beautiful thing because that's what caused Ashford Jordan the intellectual investor, to make the biggest mistake of his forty-seven years of living. "Spoon feed me? Justin is merely my watch dawg. Yes, he usually handles my legal business, but my money is my money."

Snow smiled successfully, but to Mr. Jordan, it was more suggestive. "What do you have in mind?" He asked inquisitively.

Snow seductively walked over to him and place the computer in his lap. It was a hilarious sight to see the multimillion-dollar investor, with his slacks down at his ankles and a computer in his lap.

"What better way to invest your money into a lucrative venture and have your cocked sucked all at once?" She whispered as she reclaimed her previous position.

"Well, I don't know, Ms. Waynebrook maybe we should wait for-ahhh—Ms. Waynebrook!" He couldn't even finish his sentence, Snow had his now re-erect penis gripped between her small fist. She jacked him off as she kissed his purplish head.

Between licks and kisses, she whispered. "That's—the—account. That—I—" She allowed a few inches into her mouth, held it there, and sucked as she allowed her tongue to taste the precum leaking from his nature. Then she slowly slipped it out of her mouth with a pop. "I want you to transfer the fund to that account." Snow turns her attention back to the task at hand, she takes him back into her mouth and swallows him whole.

The speed she applied took him over the edge. Her eyes never left his as his fingers began stroking the keys. Bliss captured his mind, and if he was a stronger man, the account that flashed across the screen would have revealed the meaning of the strange feeling now masked by the essence of euphoria. Everyone knew the Cayman Islands was the safe haven for a crook's treasures, now it held Brain's as well, two-point-three million dollars' worth, to be exact.

Chapter Six
Forbidden Attraction

Destiny Kendricks' hadn't been to a club in almost three years. Why would she? She was a married woman, but between the distress of her parents constant nagging of her never going back to Sa'Mage and Sa'Mage's consistent calls, she was going crazy. Making it easy to accept her cousins, Tammy and Falisha's invite to the opening of Club Dreams. Now as she sat at the table with her youngest cousin, Tammy she began to regret her desperate decision.

Destiny was dressed conservatively, in a yellow Banana Republic tube dress, a pair of four-inch nude stiletto heels, and a yellow head wrap completed her assemble. She watched her eldest relative, Falisha dance with some dude, whose hair was in cornrows.

"Oooh, she's so nasty. Look at how her nasty ass is all over that dude," Tammy said in disdain.

Destiny laughed out loud. "Leave my girl alone, she's just getting her groove on."

Tammy frowned at her sister. "More like getting her fuck on. So, what's been going on with you, Mrs. Thang? You are going to divorce that lame, ain't you?"

Destiny rolled her eyes. "Aren't, not ain't," she corrected. "I don't know if I'm divorcing 'Mage, just yet. I just don't know! I still love him he's my—ummm, my situation." She frowned at the fact that she couldn't respect calling him her husband. "I just don't know, right now."

Tammy couldn't stomach her older cousin's lack of heart. "Bitch, is you crazy? This dude allowed you to be kidnapped by some thug, ass niggas, that coulda killed you. What type of man would allow that shit to take place at home? You need to leave his bitch ass. I always told you, you need a ruff neck in yo' life."

Destiny looked at her cousin like she had two heads. "Tammy maybe that's why you're always single. Then when you're in a relationship, you're always getting your ass kicked. So, how can you enlighten me about a man, when your definition of one is a bum, that drives a 745 BMW. But, still lives at home with his mother? Girl please, I am a successful arts agent. What would I look like showing up to a gallery with a forty-year-old man who still thinks it's cool to have his pants hanging off his ass? I'd rather not, Sa'Mage may not be perfect, but he's all man. You need to get your shit together before you start giving me advice."

Tammy couldn't believe she'd just put her on blast like that. "Now hold up, you stuck up bougie, bitch! I was simply trying to be a friend and offer my advice. You know what? On second thought, you've always been spoiled. Always had your nose in the air, like your shit don't stink. Really tho— really, fuck you, D."

Destiny smiled at her relative's anger. Emotions always told the truth and as she digested Tammy's words she now understood, why she'd always distanced herself from her female relatives. Jealousy, envy, and hate is a deadly concoction, that will taint the heart of any mu'fucka, who sipped from its essence. Destiny grabbed her Tory Burch clutch purse and stood to leave.

"I'm sorry, you feel that way, Tam." Heated tears began to swim in her eyes.

She placed the oversized square framed pair of Dolce's on her face before Tammy could have the pleasure of witnessing how much her words affected her.

Tammy pinched the bridge of her nose as the stress she'd been harboring all week came crashing down. As Destiny began to walk away, Tammy's heart called out to her, "Des—Des—Des, wait." Destiny stopped but didn't turn around. "I'm—I'm, so sorry, cousin. All that stuff I said was emotional baggage that's been having me PMS'ing. You've always been my favorite girl. We're like sisters I didn't mean to upset you. It's just when you made me look at my own situation—I guess, I just lost it. The truth hurts and everything you said about me was true." Her own tears now clouded her vision.

"Tam, we've never been like sisters. Whether you meant those words or not, words spoken can never be taken back. I won't hold a grudge, you're family but it still hurts, because you know how soft my heart is. I forgive you, little cousin."

Destiny turned and headed for the door. Just as soon as she was about to make her exit, a waitress cut her off.

"Excuse me, Miss—I can see, you're about to leave. But, you have an admirer, who bought this drink for you. He also tipped me very well to make sure you got it, and this note." She handed Destiny a Sex on the Beach along with a folded napkin.

"And whom do I owe my appreciation for going this far just to get my attention?" Destiny asked.

The waitress pointed to the VIP Section, but the table she was pointing to was empty, except for a bucket of ice chilling a bottle of champagne.

The waitress seemed bewildered. "I swear he was just there—he was—" she stopped short and a smile kissed her lips.

Destiny stared at her confused and perplexed. The waitress simply pointed indicating someone was behind her. Destiny turned to find a God standing before her. His attire consisted of a burgundy, New Era hat, that sat so low on his head, you could barely see his eyebrows. A burgundy Gucci dress shirt, a pair of white Gucci shorts hanging slightly off his waist, adding edge to his appeal.

To make his ensemble complete, a four-hundred-and-ninety-dollar pair of Pierre Hardy leather high tops adorned his feet. They were burgundy, with white soles a perfect addition to his outfit. A diamond encrusted key pendant, glistened from the forty-inch Cuban link, hanging admirably from his neck. But, it was the two-tone Aviator shades concealing his eyes, that enflamed curiosity as they studied one another.

"Um, thanks for the drink and the ughh—" she stared at the folded napkin. "The umm—napkin."

The God smiled at her. The bottom row of his teeth was an indication that thirty racks was nothing to fuck off. Normally, mouth jewelry was a complete turn off for Destiny, but this God standing before her was putting on for the black brothers. His aura couldn't be denied. Destiny took a ladylike sip from her glass. Usually, she didn't indulge in drinking anything other than a glass or two of wine, but the night held her captive and she desperately needed an escape from her thoughts.

"I'm usually not a man of many words, but from the moment I set eyes on you tonight. I knew I had to step outside of my sense of ordinary if I wanted to get your attention. My truths are either going to scare you away, or you'll simply respect me for my realism." He broke the silence.

Due to the music being loud Destiny couldn't understand what he was saying, she stepped closer allowing the stranger into her space. "I couldn't understand you over the music. What did you say?"

The stranger gently wrapped his arm around her waist and slightly pulled her into him. Before she could protest his lips were lightly brushing against her ear as he whispered words into her soul, causing her to become confused, wet, and appalled.

"Ever since I kissed you there, I've found it hard to control my nature. Maybe it's the animal in me that has me fiending for your essence and yearning for your attention. I don't know what it is, but that night you stared into my eyes, I knew you felt it too."

All at once, fear, and pleasure stirred a hurricane inside of her. The voice, the height, his aura. It was the same attributes she'd been analyzing in her dreams. The same attributes causing her to question her sanity. In sequence, the glass slipped from her hand, the room became too small, her fear became morbid and recognition evaded her senses. Her knees became weak as her mental began to overwork itself.

She wanted to scream but knew she wouldn't be heard over the loud, obscene music.

Her thoughts ran wild. *'Why didn't I just stay home? What does he want? Is he here to finish me off? Why is my pussy so damn wet?'*

The stranger could feel her tremors as they raced through her body. He basked in her fear, lust, and realization. It angered him, that even after he'd kill a man for touching her, she still felt the need to fear him.

"Ms. Lady—please don't fear me. My gangsterisms has so many boundaries when it comes to you. I'd never hurt you and if nobody else knows that truth, you should."

Destiny moved with caution, as she unwrapped herself from his embrace. To her surprise, he didn't put up the least bit of resistance. Surprising even herself, she slowly reached up and slid his stunna shades off his face. As she gazed into his exotic colored eyes, heat rushed to her cheeks, and her mind took her back to the dimly lit room she shared with a dead man.

Standing before her was none other than her kidnapper, her savior, the man that killed for her.

"Look—I know this shit seems crazy, maybe even sick. But, I can't get you off my mind—" He never finished his sentence.

'Poow!' Destiny slapped him so hard his thoughts became unscrupulous. "Do you have any fucking idea what you've done to my world? Do you think this is some type of amusement to your juvenile ego?" She stared at him incredulously. "Is this some type of game? Are you some type of amateur or something? This is unbelievable!"

The stranger eyed her intensely rubbing the spot she'd just assaulted. He tried to bring some rationality to a situation, that couldn't be explained after the sin was already committed. "Dig this, lady—I know, that I could—"

'Smack!' Another slap caused fire to ignite in his eyes. His first instinct was to grab her by the throat and squeeze the fire outta her, but common sense saved him and her from his animalistic nature.

"Don't—ever put your fucking hands on me like that. I understand you're upset. In all honesty, I don't even know why I'm standing here admitting my identity to the one mu'fucka, that can get me five to ninety-nine years. It's just that I can't—I can't get you—man, fuck this punk shit." He pushed passed her and walked out into the night.

Destiny stood motionless. "Excuse me, Ms. are you, okay?" A slim, brown-skinned brother asked, as his gaze traveled from her to the shattered glass giving reality to a nightmare she was desperately trying to awake from.

"Huh, what did you say?" she questioned perplexed.

"I asked if you were alright," the brown-skinned brother repeated.

Destiny knew she must've looked like the dead, yet she asked the rhetorical question anyway. "Yes, I'm okay. But, why do you ask?"

The man thought before he spoke. '*Maybe I shouldn't have stopped for this, Sista. It's apparent she's a couple fries short of a happy meal.*' "Well—you're blocking the exit, with a crazed look on your face, and shattered glass at your feet. Not to mention, you have tears running down your pretty face."

Destiny placed her hands to her face. She had no idea, she'd allowed rain to fall from her eyes. "Oh my, God—I can just imagine how crazy, I must look. It's just that—oh, never mind. I'll be okay." Destiny turned on her heels and did the stupidest thing she'd ever done in her twenty-six years of living. She ran after her kidnapper.

***

Assata reversed his G-5 Benz truck into the only empty parking space available. It was a beautiful, Sunday evening in the nutty city of Denton, Texas. Fred Moore park or '*Fred Mo*' as natives called it was packed to capacity, with ballers, gangstas, women, and children. Assata sat reclined inside the spacious luxury vehicle as six clarion screens illuminated the tinted windows.

MO3's newest hit '*Always Be*' blasted from the eighteen-inch speakers, causing the reclined butterscotch seat to massage his muscular back. All eyes focused on the twenty-six-inch big heads glistening under the radiance of the sun.

"Naw, I can't cuff no hoe and damn, sho I ain't wifin' shit/ if it ain't just 'G' down yo' throat, then yo' chips is all I can

get/dig this-you gone hold me down bitch, when times get this/you gone be around if I go broke and I can't buy you shit—" he sang along with the verse.

Every nigga in the park glared at the luxury machinery encasing the gangsta's orbit. Niggas knew how the God that sat behind tint fucked around. He was the typa nigga, that would push a nigga's wig back for disrespecting him, then attend the same nigga's funeral simply to pay respects to the man's family. Not to mention, his squabble game was fierce. Him and Shy's rep spoke for itself, even after Shy's demise.

Even though Assata moved solo, niggas still treaded lightly, while in his cipher. Every bitch present felt the power he radiated. His presence sent tension, hate, lust, as well as fear in the atmosphere. Yet, regardless of what was going on around him, he reclined unfazed, ruling his emotions. The truest sense of a black man flowed from his pores fearless like the men of the Mandingo Tribe. His presence heightened the moment.

About fifty feet from the truck four young women, stood to the side of the basketball court, watching as sweaty niggas ran up and down the pavement doing their best impersonations of the And-1 Mixtape. Jazzy stood out amongst the foursome. Her skin looked as if she'd been tanning under the sun on an exotic island. His eyes changed colors as she stared out at the aggressiveness being exuded on the blacktop. Her plump ass and shapely thighs filled out the pair of stretch Oscar Delarenta Jeans that hugged her every curve, to top it all off the fact that, she knew she was a boss bitch sealed the deal.

Marcella her best friend elbowed her. "Um, bitch, ain't, that your boy's truck over there?"

Turning to get a better look Jazzy's eyes became slits as she observed a thick, dark-skinned girl leaning into the driver's side window. Even though, her and Assata wasn't an item she couldn't stop the feeling surging through her. Jealousy was an uncomfortable force when speaking in terms of someone, who one feels should belong to them. Although, Assata wouldn't so much as kiss her lips ever since the emotional night at her brother's grave, they'd been vibin' on the phone day and night.

To her, that meant progress in the right direction. This only made her feel bad about communicating with his enemy, Nutz. It wasn't like they were doing anything. Nutz was just her playa potna, that she'd always be cool with because he was a real nigga. But she knew Assata wouldn't dig that he's always been a protective man. He would never respect a female associating with another nigga. Friends or not. In his eyes, she might as well had been fuckin' him, cause ultimately that's where it would lead.

Since she didn't belong to either man, she didn't see a problem, kickin' it with a nigga. She was bossy and would never carry herself like a hoe.

"Yeah, that's Assata, but he's not my boy," she replied rolling her eyes at her girl.

She turned her attention back to the game, but she wasn't fooling anyone let alone herself.

Marcella continued staring as the chocolate girl flirted with Assata. Her shorts were so short her ass cheeks practically hung out of them.

"Tasteless, bitch," she murmured.

Gracy made the third wheel of the foursome. "Hump, you ain't never lied, girl." She added gazing at the G-5 lustfully. Six pairs of eyes landed on her. "What?" She exclaimed noticing the gaze. "Jazzy, telling the truth, he ain't no boy. That nigga, Assata's—all man with his black ass." She looked at Jazzy. "I'll snatch his crazy ass up if you don't want him, Jaz."

"Bihhh, please, I have the best friend privilege. So, I get dibs on his sexy ass first," Marcella interjected.

Laughter escaped everyone except, Jazz. Ignoring their banter, she reluctantly, returned her gaze to the chocolate girl now sliding into the passenger's side of the truck. Enough was enough, it seemed as if her feet had a mind of their own, as she made her move in their direction.

"Jazz, where you going?" Tessa fourth and most diplomatic of the group asked.

Marcella laughed, "Shid, she going to get her man," she said as she began taking off her earrings.

Assata was just about to put the truck in drive when the passenger door flew open.

"What the fuck?" Chocolate exclaimed staring at the cinnamon-skinned, beauty, interrupting her flow.

"No offense, cutie, but you have to raise up outta this truck," Jazzy said.

Chocolate stared at her thinking she needed to simply go away. Noticing this girl's disregard Jazzy decided to take another approach, "Bitch, if you don't get your fake, Kelly Rowland, lookin' ass up outta this truck, I'm going to snatch yo—"

'Baamm!' Before her sentence could be completed, the chocolate girl shot a quick one to her lips.

"Bitch, back the fuck up off, me."

At that moment all hell broke loose.

***

Destiny stood outside the nightclub staring bewilderedly into the night. *'Where could he have disappeared to that quickly?'* Just as the question entered her mind, a black BMW

645Ci pulled to the curb about four feet in front of her. The valet stepped from the 6-series coupe and awaited the owner.

From behind her, a baritone voice caused her to get nervous. "Curiosity is a strange notion, sometimes it can be a good thang, and other times it can be bad."

"Well, in this case, which is it good or bad?" she countered.

Her strange addiction stepped from behind her, and over to the valet holding his door open.

"Good lookin', homie." He reached inside his pocket and pulled out a bankroll. He peeled fifty from the huge stack of his bills and handed it to the young attendant.

"Preciate it, O.G. A nigga need this."

Nodding his head as a response Nuts turnt his attention back to Destiny. "You come here with somebody?"

Destiny simply stood there and stared at him. Her heart and mind were at war. Sanity and insanity danced to the melodies of rationality's limits. Without taking her eyes off of him, even though she was scared shitless.

Destiny walked to the passenger door and opened it. "Rather good or bad curiosity has gotten the best of me." She slid into the seventy-thousand-dollar car.

RENTA

Chapter Seven
Assata vs. Nutz

~Assata~

"Ooooh, shit Ass—ata—shiss damn, nigga. It ooouu, it feels like you—oouuu, fu—take it." She sang as she slid up and down my thick eight and half-inch dick.

My mind wasn't even with this bitch. Until the moment, lil' mama leaned forward, placed her hands on both sides of my head, her face in the crook of my neck, and started popping her pussy all crazy. The God lost it, I'm not one of them lame ass niggas that be tellin' a bitch how good her pussy is—making shit up. If the pussy good, it's good, if it ain't I'ma tip the hoe for effort and be in the wind.

But, shorty had me grippin' her ass cheeks and biting her neck. Isolating her upper body she used her lower half to take a nigga to the place that made the strongest of niggas soft. Six raised herself up, she slid off my dick, until she had only half of it inside of her treasure, and just like that she worked me into a crazed frenzy. All the while, I was trying to pull that ass all the way back down to the base of this dick.

Lady was adamant about driving a nigga crazy. She did her, so I did me. I begin driving upwards. This only enhanced the feeling of pleasure surging through a nigga.

"Damn, ma." I finally growled. "You tryna make a nigga wife you or sumtin'?"

What I do that for? She slid off me with the quickness and took me in her mouth. My shit hit the back of her throat. Lil' mama didn't take her eyes off mine as she swallowed my spirit. Bitch sucked my soul from my body.

After my shit eased Six licked her lips and used her tongue to wipe the last drop of cum that oozed from my nature. She kissed the head and got up without saying a word. I watched her two ass cheeks bounce, as she walked into the bathroom that was adjoined to her room. She didn't close the door, so I had a clear view as she sat on the toilet and pissed. A nigga had to smile at her audacity. The bitch was a live female and definitely a paper chaser.

She was a yellow bone, long hair don't care chick, with a light blush of freckles kissing her face. Her chestnut colored eyes sealed the deal. Standing 5'7 and weighing one-hundred, seventy pounds made her just my kind of bitch. She was a dancer at Club Pearls the way her curvaceous frame worked the stage, elevated her to the status of being 'that bitch' of the establishment.

After wiping her pussy and washing her freshly manicured hands, she made her way back to the bed with a soapy warm towel. She strode her sexy ass over to me, took my flaccidness into her hand, and began wiping me down. I reached over to the nightstand, grabbed the half-smoked blunt and lighter, and put flame to the drow as my mental strayed once again. All I could think about was Jazzy's lil' sexy ass.

Why she had to come back? Okay—I'm trippin', I know she had to come back to show love to, fam. But, why she had to come back so grown—so womanly? See a nigga will fuck a hoe all day long, but when that one bitch comes around, that one bitch, a nigga knows is built to last. That one, that stands on loyalty and morale, a nigga will change the game for her. That shit is rare and Jazzy stirred something in me that no other bitch had before.

Noticing, my mental wasn't with her, Six did what most women do when they felt neglected.

"Assata," she whined. "What's it gonna take for you to leave this street shit behind? It's not like you hurting for loot or nothing, even if you was you know I got you."

I allowed the potent weed smoke to escape my lungs before, I answered. "Look, ma, we've been down this road befo'. You, know, how I rock out here. The grit is where you met me, but now that the dick hitting the right spots yo' emotions tryna guide you, and you wanna house a nigga." The frown on lil' one's face, let me know she wasn't diggin' my gangster-ism's, but she had to respect what was real.

"Say I 'G' for you, Six. You're everything a street nigga dreams of in regard of a good bitch. I also need you to understand this shit ain't no fantasy. This life I'm living ain't one I chose, it chose me and at any moment, I could catch a slug to my face."

Six never took her eyes from her task. The warm towel felt good against my skin, as she lifted my nuts and cleaned me completely. The tension in her body told me, she didn't like where my spiel was headed. As I reached down and grabbed the half-smoked blunt on the dresser. I could see the rain forming in the wells of her eyes. She stood in front of me holding the wet towel in the palm of her hand. Without hesitation, she grabbed the blunt from my hand and rolled her eyes in frustration, but I shook that shit off and further explained my mindset.

"At any moment, Allah becomes tired of my hustle. I can end up in front of a judge facing five to ninety-nine. With them type of numbers, how much love will you hold for me then, ma?" Snatching the blunt out of her hand, I took a deep pull from the gut, before blowing the smoke in her direction. "None, you know why? Cause nobody gives a fuck 'bout a nigga when his time is up. When a nigga time expires so does the love. So, tell me Six, why you keep comin' at me with this leave the streets shit? You gone take care of me, while I'm caged up doing thirty to forty-five years and the loot gone?"

"Yes, I will," she proclaimed.

"Fuck outta here, lady. Let me ask you this and I want a true answer. What would make you betray me, love?"

Six flung the towel at my chest and tears ran down her face. "You know what, Assata, fuck you. All I ever tried to do was show and prove to you, that I'm nothin' like these other hoes out here. You already know dick nor money moves me. I'm a woman, that works for my own shit. I know how to play with my pussy better than any nigga can fuck me. All you know about me is what I reveal. You have no fuckin' idea, Assata. Honestly, I'm not 'bout to sit here, and try to convince you of my loyalty."

Rage shone in the liquid fire racing down her face, as she tried to get her point across. "And, boo, just for the record the life you're living is the life you're choosing to live. You may not have chosen it, but you've become just like every other nigga, that lives in it, institutionalized in the stigma of the hustle. The only reason you may catch a bullet to the face, or for God to become tired of your hustle is because you caught the disease every nigga before you and with you has contracted. You don't know when enough is enough."

I stared at her through glassy eyes. The look painting my face spoke volumes. Six rolled her eyes. "Yeah, I am a stripper, Assata. Yeah, I display my body for niggas, that only recognize me by my ass and titties, but when it's time to quit. I bet you I won't have to be told twice."

I sat up. "When is enough gonna be enough, Six?" I stood to retrieve my belongings. I looked down at the beautiful woman that had tears drying on her pretty face. "I know that you attend the University and shit, but you're stripping because you want to, ma. You could have any job—there's plenty of jobs that don't require you degrading yourself, for niggas that put a price tag on you.

"You know a nigga will help you if you need it, but Beyoncé got you on this other shit. Dig this, Six, Beyoncé has a nigga that she'd never cross. Beyoncé has been rich half her life. She's never had to experience the typa shit we have. So, who are we to blessings? I'm just saying, love, when it comes to decisions we all have a few to make." I put my clothes on and smashed out.

After leaving Six's spot, I had some heavy shit on my mind. Yeah, I was driving a G-5 and had a pearl white MBZ CL-550 parked in the driveway of a two hunnid thousand-dollar home. Yeah, I rested my head on fluffy pillows and lavished myself with satin sheets, but a nigga got lonely at night. Every boss nigga knows you can't bring any typa bitch into your lion's den. That's the main reason, one side of my king size Egyptian sculpted bed stayed cold at night.

It was mad dangerous inviting strangers into your home. A nigga never knows the caliber of the bitch he loving on until he wakes up to find a masked gunman with a semi-automatic weapon aimed at his face. So, I protected my sanctuary with keen judgment and a reclusive perspective. I knew I couldn't live like that forever, but I was addicted to the kitchen. I couldn't explain the rush, I felt when I ran up on a nigga with that banana shoota. It was just the life for me.

All my niggas lived on the edge. The street shit was our religion, and we were thick as thieves. It started out with four of us, but now that my ace, Shy had returned to the soil, that left me, Gusto, and Strange. Three the hard way. Gusto was a straight killa. He actually enjoyed bustin' a nigga's shit. He was a pretty boy, nigga with a crazy ass murder game. With the ladies, he was even deadlier.

I mean that *literally* because my nigga was cursed with what we called them alphabets—H.I.V. Yet, he wasn't out there passing it around like it's cool. He was just doing him living every night like he might not see the morning.

As for Strange, he was a live wire from Fort Worth, Texas. But, he was real quiet-like, almost a mute. He was real observant and believed strongly in family values.

Strange was a tall, black ass nigga, with one green eye and the other dark brown, hence the name Strange. But those was my niggas. I trusted them and no one else.

Six had my head twisted. She wanted more than I could give. Plus, I was thinking about other shit. I couldn't believe that pussy ass nigga, Nutz was violating the game like that. That nigga had to be foolish to think he could slide through my side of town and not face the music.

We had been long-time enemies since we were lil' niggas. I was reppin' the Kreek, Piru territory, B.I.P Bleed in Peace, O.G. Rusta. This nigga Nutz was bred of Hic Street and everybody knew those whack ass niggas repped five-deuce Hoova.

Him being spotted on my side of town created a conflict of interest. Even without the ongoing beef of our hoods, our most intimate grievance against each other, derived from the most common element that set flame to beef—a bitch! The very object of my fantasies to be exact.

Jazzy and Shy had to move out of the hood with their pops somewhere on the other side of town. They had switched schools and *errythang*. They ended up going to Denton High, that's where the majority of them fuck niggas of Hic Street went. Shy ended up coming back to the block with his T-Jones 'cause he was putting on for the hood and his pops wasn't feeling him getting his 'G' on.

His old man was a devout Muslim so that shit didn't blow over too well, but Jazzy found a home there. It just so happened, that the sucka Nutz went to D.H.S as well. Even though he was three years older than her, he and Jazzy started fuckin' around. If it wasn't bad enough for her to be fuckin' around with a nigga from the other side. I flipped out when she started bringin' the sucka to the block.

In the end, he had to take that bullshit '98 Seville to the shop, 'cause, I hit that bitch with eight fireballs. This only made shit between us worse. I'm from the dirt with this gangsta shit, so I fed the flame. I've always G'd for lil' one. Jazzy has always been the type of female a real nigga dreamed about. She just needed a real nigga to love her. His mother was a fiend, and her pops was a good dude who just made mistakes. She coulda been like the rest of these bum bitches and used her pussy to catch a boss, but baby girl desired more outta life. She's one of the few females from the ruts that finished high school. If that wasn't enough she ain't got fifteen, or twenty niggas, that can testify how good or bad her pussy is.

She attended college in Cali and has always walked the loyal line. She didn't know, I sent a bankroll every month through her brother just to make sure she was good. She deserved it. Yet, even with all that said I'd never fuck with her heart. I know, I won't do shit but destroy it. I'm not ready for that lovey-dovey shit. So, I let her do her. She deserved her happiness.

My nigga Shy used to tell me, "Bro, I see the way you be lookin' at my lil' sis. Bro, you, my Ru and she's been loving you since the sandbox. Do y'all—just don't hurt my blood, fam." He made me promise not to pursue her until I was ready to settle down. Needless to say, I locked it in and till this day my word is still solid.

Make a long story short, before she left for Cali she broke it off with Nutz pussy ass, but somehow word got back to him, that she did so for me. That shit was a fabrication, but truth ain't a factor amongst enemies. It was simply another reason to aim at each other's head. Now, the hood was in an uproar and had been since Shy's death. Hollow tips had been flying and blood had been spilled.

We lost some dear niggas and they lost even more. Shit ain't safe it's going down any and everywhere. So, now I'm checking the magazine on my Mac 11, preparing to get my hands dirty. Playboy shoulda ran the light, kuz it's what just caused him his life. Word 'round town was that Ice-Berg had a hand in Shy's bloodshed. Blessed be his soul.

"I told you, Shy. I'm gonna murder all them, bitch niggas! Red Rum Ru." With that pledge, I speeded the G-5 in front of the nigga's Audi, throwin' the whip in park.

I hopped out, it was about to be fourth of July, in the middle of March death on this pussy ass nigga. I didn't notice the bitch in the passenger seat until the hollows began singing that tune. Fuck it, she gotta get it too!

***

~Nutz~

I was sitting at the light feelin' like a boss should. Rolling in my baby the Audi R8 Coupe. It ran a nigga 'bout one-hundred thirty-four stacks and some change. That's not including the loot, I laid out on the deuce-fours, the five flat screens, and the eighteens beating so hard in the trunk it felt like, I was going to crack the asphalt. To compliment my status, I had one of the baddest bitches sitting sideways on the passenger seat. This bitch was bad. She stood 'bout 5'5, with short curly hair, that wouldn't fit any other female except her, and a body outta this world. Her slanted grey eyes was covered by an exclusive pair of bubble eyed Gucci shades.

Her head was bobbin' to the sounds of *Tink's* new hit, *'Bonnie and Clyde'* stuntin' with the boss. Baby girl's name was, Jazzy. She was from the Kreek, but I met her back in my lil' nigga days. She had a nigga gone from first impression. I once thought we had something real, but there was a conflict of interest that couldn't be ignored.

A conflict of interest by the name of, Assata. That pussy boy acted like him and his team's guns was the only ones that clapped. I had seen Assata slump a nigga in broad daylight, but that didn't faze me. We went from squabblin' as lil' niggas to bustin' at each other as teens. All in all, there was no way we could coexist. Someone had to return to the earth and since my two seeds needed me to show them how to be men, dude had to be the one to die.

'Yeah, I'ma slump his ass,' I decided.

Finally, the light turned green. "Man, what the fuck?" I screamed as I pulled off.

A black on black G-5 Benz truck on some gold big heads cut me off. Caught off guard my mind didn't register what was going on until two clues snapped me back to reality quick.

The only thing going through my mind was, "Damn—who gonna take care of my sons?"

In sequence Jazzy uttered. "Oh shit, Nutz, that's Assata's truck," she panicked.

Then out stepped the devil himself. He swiftly slid out the driver's seat, and even though the Dallas Mavericks fitted sat dangerously sideways on his head, it never came off. What finally brought self-preservation into play was when I notice the big Mac11 he was aiming my way. The clip was so long it made the whole gun look fake. I threw the R8 into reverse and tried to get the fuck outta there, but I guess Assata had other plans.

RENTA

Hollow points came spitting at me in a hail of fire. The windshield shattered and glass showered me and lil' mama. I ducked down attempting my escape. I jacked the wheel hard to the right in order to turn this bitch around and that's when shit went bad for a nigga. Assata ran towards us letting his murder game speak for him. The fucked-up part is that I couldn't get to my tool. Unfortunately, turning the wheel like I'd just done, fucked me rather than helped.

My side of the whip was exposed to the slaughter. That was a big mistake, because first, my shoulder exploded, then my left arm. I could hear Jazzy screaming hysterically.

"Drive, Nutz, get us the fuck outta here." This bitch couldn't have noticed I was hit.

Finally, getting the whip back in drive. I crashed my foot on the pedal and worked the wheel. With an open shoulder and leaking arm, I got us the fuck outta the storm. Before I could give thanks to the Heavens, I took one more hit to the thigh. Thank God for small blessings, because it coulda been my head. Four minutes later, we were speeding down Moore Street. I don't know which situation caused it, but two things transpired seconds after I thought we was clear.

I looked in the rear-view mirror and low and behold, the Devil had caught up to us again. The G-5 was fast approaching and all of a sudden my whole right side locked up on me. Dizziness hit me hard, and as I started losing control, the wheel followed suit. My whole side felt like it was on fire and to make shit worse this hoe wouldn't stop screaming in my mu'fuckin' ear.

All I remember is the impact that the collision with the fire hydrant had. I remember feeling blood pour from the gash on my forehead then staring down the barrel of death.

Click—click—click!

The bitch ass nigga ran out of bullets. A small smile crept on my lips as the sound of Denton's finest tainted the air. No doubt they were on the way to me—then blackness!

***

~Detective Hunter~

That motherfucker made a fool of the entire Bureau of Investigations, the DEA, and the ATF. The last I heard the prick of a district attorney, that blew the case is now flipping burgers at the local burger joint. The son-of-a-bitch made history with the stunt he pulled. The County of Denton was still facing heat and the Bureau was still under scrutiny. It's all a fucking faux pas. It makes our great state look like a paradise for crooks to migrate. It makes us look incompetent. I am in an alliance with the Federal Bureau and the higher-ups are having a shit fest behind this fucker's disrespect.

So, I am after him diligently. At this moment, I found myself at, yet another violent crime scene. So, far there had been forty-eight shell casings retrieved within a two-block radius. Not including the three that was lucky enough to leave marks. Shame that the shooter didn't have much of an aim, because if he'd been a little more in control. He would've done us a big favor by ridding the city of the scum, that was carried away on the stretcher.

"Hey, there Hunter, how's it going, buddy?" A local cop by the name of Adams acknowledged as he walked up beside me.

I continued to stare at the bullet-riddled Audi. "Beautiful car—" I grunted.

This got a snicker or two from the blue. He obviously caught the pun, intended. Seeing as I didn't join in on the laughter Adams composed himself and cleared his throat.

"So, what brings the detective with the brass balls to a crime scene, that won't even make the front page? Last I heard you had your own practice, and you were running interface with the Bureau, along with some hot shots that work with you. Word around the station was that you and your colleague are the modern-day Alex Cross and Sampson, from those James Patterson novels."

"Media gossips, Adams. I heard the gossip as well, I just take it in stride. The partner in question isn't a partner at all. Her name is Detective Winslet and she's a Fort Worth homicide detective who helps me from time to time." My gaze returned to the punctures in the side of the Audi. There was one thing that became clear to me the perp elucidated his actions. He didn't intend for, Mr. Swanson to walk away from his car. I watched as the crime scene tech approached me.

"Detective, I got something I think you might need to see." As I turned to walk away, "Hunter!" Someone called my name.

I turned my head to Detective Winslet. "Detective Hunter." She strolled over to us with a sense of pride in her stride.

We acknowledged each other with handshakes, then her eyes went to Adams. He extended his hand in a friendly gesture.

"Adams, D.P.D."

Never the rude the epitome of savoir-faire, Winslet gripped his hand in a feminine, yet firm shake. "Winslet, D.P.D as well."

A moment of maladroit silence passed before Winslet spoke. "I've been a detective for this precinct for four years now. I know damn near every officer on our force, including the chief, Lonny Flemington. I don't believe our paths ever crossed."

Adams smiled a handsome smile. "It's probably because I recently returned from a five-year tour. Since you've only been here for four years, it's no wonder we're not familiar with one another. Yet, before I was called to duty, I walked the beat for six years at this very precinct."

Winslet turned her gaze to me. "Which explains how you two seem so chummy."

I shrugged, "Hey, he's been around." I laughed as her face became flushed.

That's what she gets for throwing her experience around. So, what do you have for me, Detective? I inquired as I re-called the way she approached.

As if, she was just remembering a smile crept onto her lips. She pulled a small notepad out of her back pocket and opened it to the section she desired, but before she spoke, her eyes went from me back to Adams. This reminded me of the disap-pointment I owed the young man. "Adams, from this moment on. This case is of federal importance. The victim is under the scope by the bureau, we can't have D.P.D interfering with our investigation. So, if you'd be so kind, would you please ex-cuse me and my partner? We have things to discuss—pri-vately. The modern-day Alex Cross and John Sampson—re-member?"

The officer grinned, then asked, "What do I tell the Cap-tain, when he asks why me and the boys pulled out of the in-vestigation?"

As if on cue, a brown Crown Vic pulled up and out stepped two plain-clothed men. You could tell who they were before the tallest of the two flashed his I.D.

"F.B.I, I'm Agent Crawford and this is my partner, James O'Malley." He then turned his eyes to me. "Detective Hunter, you mind briefing us on the situation with our boy?"

"Not at all, Crawford." I then turned to Adams. "Tell the Captain, we'll be in touch.

Chapter Eight

What Else I Gotta Do!

"Give me that honey looove/there's something in your eyes, baby,/it's telling me that you want me baby/tonight is your night/and you don't have to ask for nothing/I'll give you everything you need/so giiirrl don't be shy/ooooh, child/baby come inside/oooh/turn down the lights, there is something that I want from you/Right noooow/Give me that honey loooove/that sweet, sweet love—"

R. Kelly crooned from the surround sound echoing from the club's high-tech stereo system. The thick diva commanding the stage had the entire club hypnotized. The lights were completely off. The strobe light that danced across the stage was the only illumination used for her act. Glitter saturated her flawless skin, a pair of glow in the dark, cat-like contacts shined from under her long lashes. I was completely naked except for my glow in the dark G-string.

The clear six-inch stilettos I wore made my ass cheeks poke out further than they already were. But, it was the ten-foot Albino Boa constrictor, I danced with that made my act Class A material. There is nothing more seductive than a bad bitch with a tropical snake. It all exuded from my eroticism. Erotically I danced with the music, as dollar bills rained down on me from every angle. Yet, I was oblivious to the downpour.

Like a lioness, I stalked my prey. As my green eyes landed on the entrée of my desires. I rolled my belly like a professional belly dancer. All the way down I rolled and swayed until I was on my knees in this same position. Then I crawled over to my delicacy. He was seated at the far end of the stage. Diamonds glistened from his neck, ears, wrists, and mouth.

Gossip amongst the strippers was that he was a true bred from New York with a lot of loot to fuck up. Like a goddess,

I positioned myself directly in front of him. Our eyes met through the darkness the boa gently constricted, as it crawled outward towards the man of the hour.

Unfazed by the serpent he never took his eyes away from mine. As I switched positions I placed my pedicured feet on each side of the stage, with my legs spread, as I sat my juicy pussy in the out-of-towner's face. Even through the darkness, he was able to see the wetness glistening from my partially exposed feminine lips.

'Let's go to the mall baby/I'll pick you up around three/don't you worry about a thaang.' R. Kelly continued serenading the atmosphere.

As if, the snake knew what to do it slithered down my belly making its descent to my garden of Eden. As if we were the only two present, I allowed my hands to fondle my C-cup breasts. I passed my navel and the head of the boa hovered slightly above my treasure. Its tongue tasted the sweaty air, as its red eyes studied its surroundings.

Anticipation thickened the air, as I used my right index finger to travel down my thighs until it landed upon my engorged clitoris. I massaged it gently moaning in self-pleasure. Four minutes before the end of my act, I decided to take it to the next level. The snake slid his head under my G-string as I pulled the thin material to the side exposing my freshly waxed pussy. The snake tasted my ecstasy, as a long moan escaped from my lips, and cum shot from my essence. Without warning my nectar splashed against his lips.

Once the song ended I righted myself and crawled over to the New Yorker.

I used my fingers and smeared cum over his lips before saying, "Meet me at the exit in fifteen minutes." Quickly, but with flair, I made my departure.

***

~**Six**~

As I walked into the dressing room after my set. The life of what I yearn to escape hit me straight in the face. First came the now familiar smell of sweat and a hundred different perfumes. Then all eyes focused on me. I could feel jealousy all around me.

'*These hoes are so lame. Ever since I started at this bitch ass club these hoes been hating on me.*' I thought.

As I walked over to my station, my eyes landed on the dingy bitch that had her sweaty ass cheeks in my chair.

"Isis, I'm not in the mood for your bullshit, tonight. So, please just get out of my seat."

The bitch gave me a look like I was bothering her, then turned her attention back to Honey. The girl stationed next to me. "As I was saying, girl, before I was rudely interrupted by this nobody—" she began but that is as far as she made it before my tolerance ran out.

Straight to her eye is where my fist landed. But, it was the hook I sent to her temple, that made the bitch get some sense and guard her grill.

"Bitch, I said get out of my seat!" No time to waste, I reached over, grabbed a fist full of the hussie's weave, and drug her airheaded ass out of my chair. I guess she had no other choice, but to begin swinging wildly.

So, with my free hand, I went to work on that ass. My uppercuts slowed her ass down real fast. I thought the bitch was getting tired and truthfully, I was too. I released the hoe's fake ass hair and landed one more blow before she could raise her head all of the way up. That will show a bitch that a true Dallas bitch is real about her shit.

Then, *'Baam!'* The bitch swung a wild, ugly hay-maker dazing me. Then the hoe charged me, that move wasn't one she should've made. Our impact drove us into the vanity behind me. The Mexican girl, that was standing there had to rush out of the way to avoid getting run over.

"Aagghhh," I groaned as my back crashed into the mirror shattering the glass.

Jagged pieces rained down on us. Luckily it didn't cut us until I snatched up a nice size piece and slashed the bitch across her fugly face. She screamed and grabbed her wound. Blood poured from her face like a faucet. She began screaming hysterically. I commenced to putting my foot in her ass. Out of my peripheral, I saw the intentions of 'Wet-Wet' another dancer I didn't much care for.

Her and Isis are road dawgs, so I knew she was fucked up about the ass whooping I was giving her. But, right as I was about to give her, her chance.

My best friend, Mi'Shay stepped up to the plate. "Bitch, if you try anything other than standing still. I'm going to beat that ass."

Everybody knew Mi'Shay meant every word. Bitches around here feared her, she was known inside and outside of the club for beating a bitch. Finally, Isis fell to the ground, then another problem occurred. The door to the dressing room flew open. Bull and Gucci stepped in, Bull was one of the many bouncers that ran security, but Gucci was the owner.

He stood with a toothpick hanging from his mouth. Gucci looked from me, then to Isis who was still on the ground moaning and holding her face. Then he turned his eye to the destruction left behind from our mayhem.

In his deep southern drawl he said. "Now, I'm not concerned about how much it'll cost to fix Isis's face. Hell, I'm not even concerned about why the fuck you bitches have problems. What I am concerned about is which one of you hoes, is going to pay me for the mirror y'all broke? Y'all clean this shit up and before you leave. Six, find your way to my office and stop bleeding all over my damn floor." He turned and walked out.

Bull stared at all of the bare titties like he'd never seen them before. He winked at me, then turned and followed Gucci's departure.

I looked down at my bleeding hand, I must've cut it when I grabbed the jagged piece of glass.

Before heading to the shower, I spit on Isis's bitch ass. "Stupid, bitch—all this over a fuckin chair."

***

~ Destiny~

I stood over a sedated, Nutz. His slow breathing made it seem as if he was at home in his own bed, rather than laid up heavily drugged in a hospital room. What happened to land him in his current predicament still had me quite curious, even shook. My mind wondered what this man did for a living. What all was he into? Outside of kidnapping and trying to seduce his captives. I'm sure he's a major player in the streets.

The foreign cars, the five-hundred-dollar pair of shoes, as well as the jewelry all added up to one thing—money. Blood money from my perspective. Yet and still, his swag was different from my idea of what the streets bred. He had etiquette. His mannerisms were that of a boss. Yes, his aura was that of someone you didn't want to cross.

"Oh my, God. Why am I even here?" I asked for the sixth time since I arrived.

"Ma-maybe, you—" I jumped when he spoke.

"You're awake! I'll go get the nurse," I said as I began to head for the door.

"No," he said hoarsely, "I don't need no nurse."

His face winced, as he reached for the glass of water, that was apparently left for this reason. I watched as he sipped it slowly.

"You sure you don't need a nurse?" I asked curiously.

He gazed at me through lidded eyes studying me, then placed the glass back on the stand. "Yes, I'm sure. But, you can come over here and help me sit up." He grimaced trying to upright himself.

"Oh, Lord, hold on—let me help you," I spoke, rushing over to assist this strange creature, that I found myself intrigued with. I used the controls attached to the bed and pressed up as the bed began to rise.

It put him in a sitting position. "Argh, shit," he exclaimed.

I stopped and stared at him apologetically, "Sorry."

"Nah, ma, you good 'preciate you." I smiled at his vernacular. He studied me once more. "What are you doing here?"

I couldn't really give him an honest answer. Hell, I didn't know the answer. I just gave him the only honest answer, I could give.

"Well—um, an officer contacted me while I was at work and told me you'd been shot. He said the reason he contacted me was because he was going through your phone looking for an emergency contact and found my number under—um, wife."

Our eyes locked as I waited for him to clear the air, yet all he said was, "Stop avoiding the question, Destiny. Why are you here? Not how you got here—not who contacted you. But, why did you come?"

Releasing a long gush of wind, I finally had to admit the truth. "I—I don't know," I whispered as I turned to get the hell out of there as fast as I could.

Before I could take the slightest step in the opposite direction, he reached out and gently, yet firmly latched on to my wrist. I turned to face him stubborn tears welled up in my eyes. Confusion, anger, lust, curiosity, and anticipation—it was all part of my insanity at this very moment.

Just this morning I had my family's lawyer contact Sa'Mage. He should be receiving the divorce papers in a few days. He refused just as I thought he would. But, my lawyer informed him, that if he decided to take this in front of the courts, we'd not only win but also clear him out. Sa'Mage wasn't a stupid man by far. He knew if he stood before any judge in the state of, Texas. He'd undoubtfully lose and have to pay alimony. So needless to say, he ended up conceding.

'Please don't confuse my actions with my emotions.' I love Sa'Mage this man is attentive, loving, responsible and dedicated. It's just that his profession has caused us one too many problems on the home front. It's not safe with him anymore. This last incident was the last straw to add salt to the wound. I was standing in the presence of the very man, that help create the rift in my marriage.

That night at the club I left with him and he took me to a beautiful place surprising even me. He drove us to a spot located on the outskirts of the city. It was a splendor, a cliff that had a sixty-foot drop into a celestial lake. From our location, we could see the airport. For a second, we simply fell in love with the silence, as we followed the descent and departure of the aircrafts.

Then out of our moment of silence, he asked me. "If you could just pack your shit and aboard one of those planes—where would you go?"

Without looking in his direction. I answered, "Egypt!"

"Why Egypt?"

I continued to gaze at the beautiful invention that defied gravity. Then moments after his question, I gave him my reason for yearning.

"To visit the North-Eastern part of, Africa. It's a beautiful country on the Mediterranean. It's the homeland of the mighty, Queen Nefertiti and King Ay, who was known as God's Father. Which in some cases can simply indicate its bearer being the father of a queen. But, for more of an ancestry of the people and the wonders they created. I just want to go back to where it all began. Not simply our ancestors but our knowledge—our power. Home," I whispered. "It's the home of our people." Then I verbalize what we both knew but evidently forgot. "James—I mean, Nutz, I'm married."

What happened next surprised me for the third time that night he began to strip. Once he was down to his boxers, he opened the car door. I was appalled, I knew this negro didn't think he was getting any.

Before I could cuss his ass out he replied, "I know." He slid out of the 6-series and before he did the unthinkable, he turned around and stared at me through the illumination of the headlights and tinted windows.

"Escapism," he said.

The crazy muthafucka plunged sixty feet into the dark reflecting water.

"Escapism." A perfect word for my current actions. An attempt to forget reality through fantasy.

***

~Six~

My pussy was now cleaned, but my hand throbbed from the thirteen stitches used to seal the jagged cut from the jaded glass, courtesy of Denton Regional Hospital. The out of towner whose name is, York drove me to a modest flat he stayed at when he was in town. As we pull up to the apartment building my cell phone rang. Reluctant to answer, I allowed voicemail to pick up the call.

"What's good, ma? That yo' nigga or sumin'?" York questioned.

I giggled a little and replied. "And what if it is? I'm here with you, Daddy."

Seeming content he said. "Right—fuck dude, ma. You, wit' a true God, now."

Little did he know this Samsung was a throwaway. I allowed voicemail to pick up because the caller would hear me informing him all was a go and the door to the apartment would be unlocked. Sexy as he was York was simply flossing too hard around the wrong type of niggas. We'd been on him for about two months now. We knew all about playboy's business. The ten gauges he kept under the couch. The four bricks he had disguised in flour bags. We even knew about the forty stacks he had stashed safely in the safe, hidden inside the big screen television.

Actually, from what I heard the T.V. wasn't a T.V. at all. It was merely the T.V. frame. *'Who in the fuck thinks like that?'* I know so much about dude's honeycomb hideout because he has that sickness most niggas who ain't used to having shit catch after they stumble on a few pennies—diarrhea of the mouth.

There are four things in this cruel world that will make a weak nigga run his mouth as if he was drunk. One some wet pussy, two some fire head, three a pistol in his face, and last but not least an interrogation room full of federal agents and a little pressure. As for this boy York, it was the fire head from my girl Mi'Shay that made him spill the beans.

All it took was two nights of freaking for him to start bragging 'bout the loot and drugs. What gives niggas the impression, that a bitch will respect them any differently. I don't have the slightest idea, but in this case, I'm glad, York was foolish enough to reveal his hand to a scandalous bitch like Mi'Shay. She was always down to make a quick dollar, so when she told me how this nigga was running off at the mouth. I passed the info to 'my boo' and here I stood.

Willingly ready to suck, fuck, whatever my baby needed to add to his ways of life. What else I gotta do to prove to this nigga I was built to be his queen?

**

~Assata~

Sticking to the shadows of the apartments. Gusto, Strange, this nigga Fiya a young stick up kid from around the way, and myself made our way towards York's spot. We'd been waiting for this nigga for quite some time. With gloved hands, I gripped the MPS tightly. With a quick glance behind me, I noticed my niggas, masked up, in all black, clutchin' weapons that should be illegal to niggas of our caliber.

Just around the corner three doors enclosed somebody's privacy and protected somebody's treasures. Behind these three doors, somebody felt safe. Power surged through me, as the anticipation of the unknown enhanced my senses. My eyes locked onto the door in the middle breezeway.

"Showtime, my niggas!"

***

~Six~

Ecstasy was the only word that could be used to describe the way I was feeling at the moment. But, before I put you onto why I'm on the verge of cumin' all over my best friend's lips. Allow me to bring y'all up to speed on how I ended up straddling Mi'Shay's face as York fucked her like he had a point to prove.

Let's backtrack a few hours. Once we got to his apartment, York was all over me. I wasn't trippin' 'bout the four-play. I wasn't even trippin' when he pulled me close to him, slipped his hands behind me, and cupped my bare ass cheeks. His jeweled hands lifted my skirt so that it sat on top of my plump ass. As he massaged my money maker, he sucked my neck at the same time. While he did his thing I wondered, what he'd do if he knew he was merely getting my pussy wet for another nigga's dick to slide up in it.

Then the craziest shit entered my mind. How did I end up as a stripper, that set niggas up to get their shit taken? I wasn't raised like this. I wasn't raised to be attracted to niggas like Assata. But, I guess you can say my promiscuity derived from my strict upbringing. I grew up in a devoted Catholic home. Strict would be an understatement, really. My father wouldn't allow me to attend public school. He felt today's society of teenagers would contaminate his little princess.

My mother, uggh the woman, was brainwashed by him and the Virgin Mary's way of life. So much so, that every article of clothing I possessed growing up could've been the garments of a Monk. Long story short when I was eighteen years of age I left. As soon as, I began attending sorority parties, nightclubs, and rocking the latest fashion? Oh, my God, not to mention my first encounter with a real 'boss nigga'. That was all she wrote.

Needless to say, when my father heard about my new identity he blew the roof. He and my mother cut me off financially, with hopes of me returning to them on my hands and knees. But, the only place you'll find me on my hands and knees is at Club Pearlz. As niggas pop bands on this fat ass. Now, back to the current. York released my ass cheeks and found a different part of my body he wanted to explore. The extra tight pink wife beater, I had on did little to conceal my hardened nipples. Not to mention, I was braless.

"Wait, hold up, playboy." I finally whispered.

I brought his face to mine and peck him softly on the lips. Then I gave him the tongue. Reaching down, I found his erect dick straining against the fabric of his Akoo jeans. I grab it and dragged him over to the burgundy leather sofa.

"Sit," I demand.

I reached behind my back and unzipped my skirt. As I shimmied it down over my hips. I watched as York's eyes bore down onto the spot, that was semi-covered by the skirt. Lust, curiosity, and passion it boiled in his round browns as the skirt fell and pooled around my pedicured toes. The pink thong I had on hugged my lower lips so snuggly they imprinted the fabric.

"You like what you see, Daddy?" I purred and like a stupefied dog, he nodded his head. "I got a surprise for you," I said, as I walked over to my purse and retrieved my phone.

I press down on the number 5 and speed dialed the other piece to the puzzle. As I spoke into the receiver, I watched York's face turn from a look of lust into a look of concern.

After I ended my call, I smiled at him seductively. "You don't have any music in this bitch?" I asked as my eyes landed on the surround sound entertainment center.

Ignoring my question, York's paranoid ass got off the couch and headed in my direction. "Who was that, ma? You on that stick-up shit or what, huh?" His sudden change in demeanor shook me a little. "What—what are you talking about, York? I just told you that—"

'Bam—bam—bam!' The knocks at the door stopped me short.

"Go answer the door." He said, then reached under his shirt and came out with a nickel plated .380. He aggressively pushed me towards the door.

"What the fuck is wrong with you, nigga? Are you, manic depressive or something?" I screamed as I stumbled towards the door, with the crazy nigga right on my heels. As I opened the door, York pushed me out of the way and aimed the .380 at the person standing there.

"Wha—what the fuck?" Mi'Shay said staring down the barrel of the pistol.

A perplexed look crossed, York's face as his eyes roamed over her 5'9 frame. Then he scrutinized her attire, a long string of pearls hung from her neck. The Burberry trench coat she sported was tied in front, yet the cleavage peeking from underneath made it evident she wasn't wearing any clothes.

"Damn, ma—my bad, I'm wilding, yo," he apologized as he lowered the weapon.

As the shock wore off, Mi'Shay's heart began to beat regularly. A small smile crept onto his lips as she stared at him and pulled the sash loose. As the trench parted, a perfect set of pierced titties and a trimmed cat greeted him.

"You was going to kill all of this good pussy. Before you got the chance to get your dick wet?" Mi'Shay questioned.

"Ma, I was—"

"Shhh," she silenced him with a finger to his lips. Removing her finger, she used her tongue to trace the outline of his lips.

"Y'all gonna get it poppin' right there in the breezeway? Or, y'all gonna come in and get this shit poppin' the right way?" I interrupted from the living room couch.

Mi'Shay pushed him backward into the apartment. Right before she entered behind him, she caught a glimpse of a masked face peeked around the corner.

***

~ **Assata**~

Just as she said it would be the front door was unlocked. I pushed the door open slowly. Aiming the muzzle through the small opening, I took a quick glance inside. The lights were off in the living room. I glanced behind me and nodded at Fiya with a signal. I let him know he was up next. If we were walking into a trap, and if York was a nigga that stayed on note. Fiya wouldn't be as missed as one of my main niggas, Gusto or Strange. So, he'd have to be the first one in. Like a trained Navy Seal he slid into the darkness of the apartment.

The rest of us waited for him to give us the signal before we entered. Out of the darkness, a gloved hand appeared in the shape of a 'P'. Silently, me and the goons ventured passed the point of no return. Since I was the last to enter, I shut the door behind me. My eyes fell upon the floor model big screen, that was encased within a very expensive entertainment center.

A loud, slapping noise, followed by a moan serenaded the air. "Fuck her, yes—yeeesss—ummm—eat this pussy, Shay!" I heard a familiar voice crying out.

A wicked grin formed on my lips this bitch is bossy.

***

~Six~

My juices saturated Shays lips as I began to cum for the third time. The faster York fucked her the more pressure she applied to my clit.

"Oooh, Shay—girlll, I'm— I'm—bout—uhhh, I'm 'bout to cum—fuck." I moan as honey poured from my fountain of love.

Shay licked me clean until I became too sensitive to rock in this position any longer. I had to force my face away from her deadly tongue. I turned so I could see how she was taking all the dick this Nigga was putting in her. The pussy must've been good because the nigga's eyes rolled to the back of his head. I could tell he was on the verge of nuttin' because his strokes became intense.

"Damn, ma, this—fuckkk? This shit is crazy, yo," he grunted.

"Yasss, Daddy—ooh, fuck me—fuck me, daddy," Shay purred.

I crawled over to her and took one of her engorged nipples into my warm mouth. As I sucked and gently nibbled on it, I used my thumb and pointer finger to squeeze the other one so that neither one felt neglected.

"Ooh, shit—oh shit, I'm 'bout to nut," York screamed as he pulled out of her. He began feverishly jacking his eight and half inches until he bust.

"Y'all enjoying yourselves?" Assata asked.

York reacted with the quickness of a mongoose, as he rolled off the bed and came up with the .380. He screamed aiming the gun in the masked men direction.

Mi'Shay jumped up off the bed. "Strange!" She screamed as York reached out and grabbed her back by her hair.

"Bitch, get back here," he growled. "Oh, so yo' name is Strange, huh?" He turned his attention back to Shay. "Where you was going yo', huh?" He placed the pistol to her temple. "How you know these niggas names, bitch? I'll tell you how—y'all hoes set the kid up. Yo, this hoe will catch a hot one if you niggas don't back the fuck up out of here." He yelled as spit flew from his mouth.

Then a turn of events that wasn't part of the original script transpired. Without my consent, piss escaped from me as a gunshot rang out and a pair of lifeless eyes stared at me after the body fell to the floor. What the fuck had I gotten myself into?

***

~Assata~

This bitch ass nigga held this bullshit high-point .380 to Mi'Shay's head. We simply stared as the pussy made threats like he was the one in control. I noticed that the girl ass nigga was so shaken, he didn't even notice his heat was still on safety.

"Strange," Mi'Shay screamed as tears slid down her pretty face.

I glanced at my nigga to see how he was taking this certain turn of events. I noticed him and lil' one was getting real close lately. Without warning, Strange stepped forward and aimed his Glock .40 at York's head. The infrared beam landed directly in the center of his thinking cap.

"Nigga, if you think a bitch, means more to me than getting my fam straight you a fool." Suddenly he changed his target and with precision, his gloved hand squeezed the trigger. A hollow point spat from the silencer, equipped pistol, and found its destination in the middle of Mi'Shay's forehead. Her soul escaped as her body crumbled to the floor.

York bitched up real quick. Mi'Shay's blood and brain matter stained his face. "Please, please don't kill me, yo." He dropped the bullshit .380 to the floor and threw his hands up to the air.

Gusto rushed over and slapped him across the face with the butt of the .45. Without warning, Fiya vomited all over himself. Me, Gusto, and Strange looked from him to one another.

"Weak ass nigga," I mumbled.

"Say, man—there's no need for all the physical. God—the work's in the closet and the loots stuffed inside the shoe boxes," York volunteered.

I looked down at the machinery, I held in my gloved hand. I had to laugh, cause I'd brought the MPS instead of the nine because I enjoyed the fear it instilled in niggas. Niggas saw this big head mu'fucka and knew without a shadow of a doubt shit wasn't sweet.

Without hesitation, Strange moved towards the closed closet. "Say, my G—if you fuckin' around, I'ma knock yo' shit back and storm yo' spot. So, don't be on no fuck shit. What I'ma find in this closet?" He said as he stared at the closet door.

York got nervous sweat began to dot his flesh. His silence made even my suspicions go up. Sticking his ear to the door Strange listened intently. A strange look formed on his face.

"There's somebody in there," he whispered.

I kept my eyes on the boy, York.

"Who's in there?" Gusto asked.

The hoe ass nigga switched from tuna to a shark in a matter of seconds. "Fuck y'all, niggas! Y'all niggas gonna have to murk me up in here, son. I'm Queens, nigga. Go hard or go home, Duke."

I couldn't help but laugh at his antics. This hoe ass nigga done watched State Empire one too many times, but the thing about it is this ain't Queens and it sho' ain't no movie.

Gusto laughed as well. *Phew—Phew*! The sweet sound of fireballs being hushed by a silencer flooded the room. York crumbled to the floor right next to, Mi'Shay.

"Bitch ass nigga." We all glance over at the closet. "Whoever's in this bitch, you better bring yo' ass out, now," Strange demanded.

Silenced followed so you know what followed a deadly silence. Three shots penetrated the door—then two more. Something or someone rather crashed to the floor.

"What the fuck, dawg? What you cat's, into?" Fiya screamed through the moments he wasn't throwing up.

Then, if that wasn't bad news whimpering could be heard from the other side of the bed.

"Damn," I completely forgot about, Six.

I rushed over to where she lied in the fetal position. She looked pale as she mumbled incoherently. I smelled urine, then I heard some bad shit.

"I'm so, so sorry, Mi'Shay. I—oh, God! I didn't know—I didn't know, they were killers," she cried.

***

~**Six**~

Please, Lord, don't let them kill me—please. Lord! Mother Mary, I'm sorry for—"

"Man, get the fuck up, Six. You trippin', ma," Assata said reaching down to help me up.

Surprising even myself, I began kicking, scratching, and swinging. All I could do to protect myself from what I assumed was coming. I'd seen too much.

Whaap! First, I became paralyzed with fear, secondly, the sting vibrating across my face assured me, I'd just been slapped.

"Bitch get a grip before something bad happens to you," Assata demanded. He reached down and offered me his hand. "Get up, ma."

I stared at him, trying to evaluate his intentions, but the ski mask hid his facial expressions and his eyes had no emotion.

"Please, Assata—I promise, I won't say anything—just don't kill me please, boo," I begged as tears rolled from my soul.

"Six, I'm gonna say this one more mu'fuckin' time—get the fuck up!" The impatience in his voice told me his tolerance level was getting short. "Where yo' clothes at, ma?"

Disoriented, I gaze at him perplexed, that did it. His eyes darkened, as his hand found my face, but this time he didn't slap me. He gripped my jaws a little to firmly. "Six, go find yo' damn clothes, get dressed, and wait for me in the car. If you do anything stupid, like call the cops or leave. I'll find you, wherever you're at, and rock you to sleep. Nobody is going to hurt you, ma. Chill the fuck out," he assured, but the looks Gusto and Strange was giving me spoke volumes.

They didn't want to let me leave this room alive. I spotted my clothes over in the corner, walked over, and retrieved them. In the same manner, I walked my little scary ass over to Assata.

As I begin to get dressed I looked in Assata's eyes and said, "I'm good. I'm gonna stand over here by you until you ready to leave."

He studied me with intense eyes. "You sure?"

I nodded in agreement. The truth was I wasn't 'bout to walk pass Gusto's ass. Just as soon as I did he would've shot me in the back of my head. The look he was giving me assured that.

***

~Assata~

After getting what we came for Strange opened the closet just to see if playboy was telling the truth about the other work and loot. Laid down on the floor, with eyes wide open, and blood pouring from the gunshot wounds was a massive Doberman pincher, asleep eternally.

Strange looked back and shrugged his shoulders. "He shouldna barked at me, I'ma dawg, too."

We all laughed, well, everyone but Six and Fiya. As a matter fact, Fiya sat over in the corner with a sickening look on his face. As Strange rummaged through the closet. I glanced over at my nigga, Gusto who was now eating an apple he found in York's fridge.

"Where you find this nigga at?" I asked.

He glanced over at Fiya. "Man, bro, the nigga is my lil' sista's boyfriend. The sucka always talkin' that gangsta shit, so I brought him along. Pussy ass nigga," he remarked.

Strange came out of the closet, carrying a shoe box filled to the brim with money, and about two and a half bricks of powder. "Guess the nigga was telling the truth," he smiled tossing the work and loot to Gusto to put in the bag with the remainder of our new-found fortune.

Gusto always the extremist came out of the bag with a can of lighter fluid. "Fiya, get yo lil' bitch ass over here."

Fiya stood and stumbled over to him fearfully. "Wha—what's up, Gus?"

Gusto handed him the fuel. "Pour this shit everywhere you can."

Fiya took the can of fluid with shaky hands as soon as he turned to follow orders. Gusto clobbered him over the head with the butt of his .45. Fiya fell to the floor out for the count. Gusto picked up the lighter fluid and saturated not only the room but Fiya's sleeping frame. As we made our exit black smoke was already flowing from the evidence that would soon be no more.

"Damn, I love it when a good plan comes together! Now, what the fuck am I gonna do with Six's scary ass?" I mumbled to myself.

***

~Jazzy~

Standing outside Assata's door, I'd battled with myself for the last fifteen minutes. Maybe I should just walk away! It was too frustrating all the hurt, shame, anger and emotions. It was all just too damn much. They say pressure burst pipes. That's the thought that raged through my mind, as I collapse where I stood, while tears bled from my eyes like an open wound.

"Why? Why did he try to kill, me—me!" Unconsciously, my hand reached for the door.

I don't know how long, I sat there losing my mind before I realized the door was wide open. Assata stood before me in all his sexy ass glory. In nothing but a pair of Ralph Lauren boxers that did little to conceal his deliciousness. As I tried to pull myself together our eyes lock. He observed the cuts and bruises from the aftermath of his very own gangsterism's.

Before I could pull myself to my feet, he rushed over to me, and effortlessly pulled me up. Anger took prestige and boiled over, as I scratched and punched him relentlessly.

"You tried to kill me, you black mu'fucka! I can't believe—you actually tried to—"

Using much force Assata found my right wrist and held it, until the point of pain. He pulled me into the foyer and closed the door examining me. "You're hurt! Who did this to you? Fuck you mean, I tried to kill you, Jazz?" He fired off each question with venom spewing from each word.

Fear and confusion surged within me, as I took notice of the monstrous pistol, I didn't see when he answered the door. Anger stained his eyes as his care and fire overwhelmed me. Even through my emotions, the attraction I held for this man found its way between my legs.

"You, Assata, you almost killed me," I whispered harshly as he stared at me perplexed.

***

~ Ice-Berg~

I awoke suddenly the sweet aroma of perfume had my senses alive. Yet, the problem was I stayed alone, so there shouldn't have been any other scents except my own dancing around. I quickly reached for the .40 I kept cock and ready under the opposite pillow, panic and bewilderment told the story, even before the soft voice confirmed my suspicions.

"Chu sleep as if chu safe in su casa. Chu shake hands with dangerous men. But, sleep with chu gun under your pillow, as if chu have time to grab it before enemies fill chu with bullets."

I reached over and turned on the lamp beside my bed. I tried not to allow fear to taint my face. But shid—this typa shit didn't happen every day, especially to a nigga like me. Standing before me was a deadly, beautiful creature, that even I knew shouldn't have been there. Belle held my .40 in her small hand with a grip that left me no room to doubt her experience.

"Fuck, you doing here? Bitch, you must be crazy!" I exploded trying to crawl out of my king size bed.

The look in her eyes said so much, that I reconsidered my decision and awaited her reasoning.

"Chu so vulgar and disrespectful to a woman of my caliber, if chu enjoy being alive. I suggest chu be more careful with chu tongue, si. It's a powerful little instrument, inside the bed and outside of it." She giggled to herself.

She studied me for a moment and did the craziest thing ever. She threw the pistol on the bed. I snatched it up before the pretty bitch could blink, my free hand squeezed her neck, cutting off every precious breath her lungs craved to keep her amongst the living.

"Bitch, how the fuck you get in here? Why the fuck are you here?" I hissed through clenched teeth.

I was thinking this hoe must be manic or something. Her eyes began to roll to the back of her head, yet a blissful smile creased her face. The sudden urge to jam the tool down her throat ate at me, but the sudden feeling of something hard resting against my dick told a tale of a wasted life.

"Let—go—of—me," She forced from somewhere deep.

Reluctantly, I did just that a nigga needed his nature. Stepping away from her, she gulped down mouthfuls of oxygen. The black .22 she clutched was small, but I knew size had nothing to do with the results of the fire it spat. I did what seemed appropriate, I laughed. I'd already noticed the .40 had been robbed of its clip. This bitch not only found a way into my castle but also assured I'd be at no mercy.

"Don't you ever—ever put chu fuckin' hands on me again," she growled.

"Fuck, you doing in my house, lady? You trying to get us both killed? Your husband—"

"My husband knows nothing of this. He won't find out if chu knows what's best for you," she interrupted. "Me come to ensure chu tat chu package arrived safely. I also added three more Ki's to the seven you were already promised. Me know, chu now come home and tings are—" She paused and looked around my scarcely furnished room. "Slow, should I say. So, I want to help you climb back to the level a man like chuself deserves."

This bitch had lost her fuckin' marbles. There was no way I was working for her and copping from her nigga, too.

"Look, Mrs. Lady, you've violated my space. You're holding me hostage with a .22. Your whole energy is a contradiction, that doesn't sit well with my cipher. You have my life in the balance, yet insult the God in me by trying to make me your worker." Deciding on chance, I walked past her, outta the direction of her little toy.

From the first moment, I laid eyes on this hoe, I knew she was treacherous. But, she was more than sneaky and dangerous she was suicidal. Her nigga was gonna want blood for the sins of her actions. Even tho, I was 'bout that action my pockets were too small to wage war with a kingpin, especially over a bitch. Before I could exit my room, I smashed into a stone wall, or at least I thought it was but it was just some big ugly mu'fucka, with an even bigger gun clutched in his mitts.

This bitch done brought a cause for war into my home and all I could do was watch as shit unfolded. Glancing back at her, she smiled with an innocence, that would blindfold a nigga to her true nature if he didn't know better.

"Deja Que pase el," she said.

Whatever the fuck she said must've meant get the fuck out the way. The ugly mu'fucka stepped out of the way with a quickness. Stepping into my living room my thoughts lead me to the P.89, I keep under the couch cushion. However, the MAC in homie's hand, warned me that my spirit would already be standing before, God before my hand could clutch the steel. Besides, if the hoe knew to check under my pillow in the bedroom. Then nine times outta ten the tool had already been found.

I took a quick glance at her to find her standing in confirmation. This shit was crazy. At least that was my mindset before my eyes landed on one of the most beautiful visions I'd ever seen in my twenty-six years of living. Ten blocks of raw cocaine sat on my living room table. As I scratched my head I didn't even notice, Belle had eased up beside me with the silence of a stalking cat.

"Chu eyes can never lie to me, David. Chu are a lion, that needs his own pride to protect. From the very moment, I laid eyes on chu, I knew chu were Fuerte, ambisioso! El único."

I gazed at her quizzically, like bitch you know I'm all nigga. I don't understand that shit.

Catching on she said, "Strong, ambitious. The one! Me no want chu to work for me, you owe me nada. Yet, if you are half the man I assume you to be. You'll see me beyond the nice breasts and moments of flirtation you witnessed at the poolside of me casa. Aphrodite, I think, was merely a compliment. I'd much rather be the image of Santa Muerte, the saint that me papa prays to, that his papa prayed too and—" she smiled, "—well, chu get me point, hmm."

Finally tearing my eyes away from the pyramid of promise. I figured out the point of this pretty mu'fuckas angle. "You're playing a dangerous game, Belle. You disrespect my home and offer me drugs that'll more than likely end up painted in blood. From the moment, I saw you, I knew you were sneaky and burning to dance with the devil. I don't give a fuck what you see in me. I do know you don't see a sucka.

"Now, dig this, seven of these pretty bitches are paid in full, but the extra three screams future bloodshed. Since it's your husband, you're stealing from it's your neck on the chopping block. My thing is nobody gives away one-hundred G's worth of work expecting nothing in return. So, let's cut the propaganda and talk shop. What you want from me, ma?"

For what seemed like forever we had an eye wrestling match. Until she finally lost her fuckin' mind and tested my nuts at the same time. Her face was stone as she stared me in the eyes.

"Chu are absolutely correct, blood will spill in due time. The question is whose blood will it be? I no want chu love, I want chu hands wet with the blood of my husband," she smiled. "A sacrifice to the holy death."

***

~Assata~

It's been some crazy shit popping off with me in this lifetime. But, to have my nigga's baby sister think, I tried to off her fucks with me in a crazy way.

"Fuck are you bumpin' 'bout, Jazzy?" I growled.

As rain fell from her eyes she opened a book, that crushed me to read. Even though, I'm the main character in the story. She explained how she was rocking with Nutz three days ago and someone tried to kill her. As she cried I damn near lost control, as recollection somehow transported me back to the day in question. The recoil of the MAC, as I molested the trigger, the adrenaline surged through me, as I savored the moment of twisting Nutz wig back. Then finally my thoughts landed on the bitch in the passenger seat—Jazzy.

Instinctively, I pull her to me envisioning the blood, that coulda been spilled that day, fuck. "I apologize, mama. I didn't know—I swear it, Jazz. You know I'd never bring harm to you." My soul cried as I palmed her face and studied the evidence of me putting my gangsta down.

The damage was minimal, yet anger ignited within me. "Fuck was you with that pussy for, anyway?" I seethed. "You back rockin' with, lil' daddy? That's the same nigga, the streets sayin' smoked your—damn." In frustration, I released her and punched the wall.

That shit slipped I could feel the heat radiating from her stare. Jealousy and insanity clouded my senses now I had to explain this shit.

"Wha—what did you just say, Assata? Run that shit by me again. Finish yo' statement, mu'fucka." The defiance I knew surged through her bloodstream, boiled over into her eyes.

I turned to face her—shiddd—somebody has to be the devil. Why not me? "Look, Jazz, the streets talked to a real nigga. It's being whispered, Nutz and his pussy ass brother got Shy's blood on their hands. But, we both know how the streets tell false tales. I'm not sure who wacked my dawg, but since I'm not sure. I'ma paint the city red with them, niggas, whole block." I studied her awaiting her to lose herself in her emotions. The craziness of her reaction still had me lost for words. "Forgive, me Shy—"

***

~Nutz~

Days passed since I was released from the hospital. I hadn't left the safety of my crib since I got here. The pain in my shoulder was folly. My arm had a dull ache, and the right side of my body still felt numb. But at least, I still had all my limbs, and I had a live-in nurse. Well, not live in but she's here from sun up to sun down tending to my every need.

She cleans and dresses my wounds and makes sure the kid is fed. She even bathes a nigga. Now, that's some boss shit.

"Hey," she exclaimed as if she could feel me praising her.

"Hey, yourself, mami. What's in the bag?" I asked since she acted like shit was top secret.

"Nosey much," she giggled.

"This right here is G-14 classified, but since you need to know. I got two movies, they're that ole school gangsta shit, too." She pulled the whole store outta the bag, then tossed me a bag of mini butterfingers.

"Now, that's my shit." I saluted her and tore the bag open.

She held up two movies. "*Love and Basketball* or *Menace to Society*?" she questioned.

"*Menace to Society* is the bidness we all know ain't shit gangsta 'bout no *Love and Basketball*. It's good shit, though. *Menace to Society,* hands down!" I made my pick.

She frowned her face. "Umph, just like a street dude, but it's your night. So, shoot 'em up bang-bang it is."

I watched as she headed for the kitchen. This had to be the baddest mu'fucka in the Lone Star State. She was a classic beauty who made a pair of sweats, and a wife beater look like a million-dollar outfit with no make-up needed. She returned from the kitchen, then dimmed the lights and joined me on the couch.

She tucked her feet up under her legs and faced me "Thought it was a movie night, Queen—or am I the movie?" I joked watching her watch me.

"What do you want from me, James?" The question was direct and simple. I still found myself at a loss for words.

Yeah, I felt something for her. Yeah—I wanted to fuck the shit outta her pretty ass. But, how did I tell this woman, that the life I live is filled with monsters? That loving me is deadly? But, I want her regardless?

"Feel me, ma, a man can swim the ocean, climb over a mountain, or try to build a staircase to heaven attempting to obtain something he can believe in. It's crazy because once he's earned scars and leaked his blood on different parts of the earth, just to live within the moment of holding the mu'fucka, he fought to hold—none of that shit mattered. I'm a street nigga with a dark path, Destiny. The shit I want from you can't be placed into words because it's something deep. I gotta show you what I want from you." I reached over, grabbed her hand, and pulled her to me. She flinched as I placed her hand on my bandaged shoulder.

"Destiny—this is real—these holes aren't a part of no prep for some rap video. I understand you're a winner, we are just in different worlds. So, what I want from you shouldn't be the question. What I need from you will satisfy your curiosity and apprehension."

I pulled her feet from beneath her, then Destiny straddled me, careful not to put too much weight on my wounds. Our lips were inches apart. "Well, what do you need from me, Nutz?"

Destiny had me hard as a rock and I threw caution to the wind. I kissed her as if life was ending any second. As I pulled away slightly, the truth slid from my lips with hopes of not getting rejected.

"I need your life, Destiny. Your love, loyalty, your trust— I need your life, ma."

***

~Jazzy~

Sweat dried on our skin as we laid there spent from some real animalistic shit. This nigga was a beast in the sheets. Even though, I hadn't had many sexual partners. I couldn't imagine anyone with a deadlier stroke.

"Assata—Assata," I repeated. "Stop acting like your ass sleep. Don't you think we have something to talk about?"

His eyes opened slowly and just the way this man gazed at me, made me want to make sweet love to him again and again.

"Yeah," he responded "Why the fuck was you in the car with that lame? Let's start there and the rest will fall in place."

Instantly, I got defensive. No one knew me and Nutz relationship. Not even Nuts himself. Truth be told, I loved Nutz in a sick kinda way. Assata is my childhood fantasy! I've always had fire for him, but he would never even consider giving into me. I wanted this man to the point of insanity, but he shunned me like the plague. That typa shit cracked a girl's confidence, that's exactly what happened to me.

When my brother moved back with our moms. I was all alone with a father that meant well, but was spitting shit I wasn't trying to hear. So, when me and Nutz met not only was it a confidence booster, it was also an opportunity to make Assata see he wasn't the only gangsta in the world.

Long story short, a game turned into something real as I realized some of the same attributes Assata possessed so did Nutz. Over time Nutz became my generic version of the man my heart yearned for so much, that I fell for his thuggish ass, and gave him my virginity. My heart still beats for, Assata. Seeing Nutz again awoke my feelings for him. Only long enough, for me to realize a substitute only ignites the desire for the real thing.

How do I explain that to this man? I exhaled. *'Just keep it funky with him'*. I thought. "Assata—you know me and Nutz used to rock. I ain't spoken for, so I saw no ill will kicking it with him. I know y'all don't like each other, but I'm not part of that life. You're out here living as if you're in a Western movie. You tried to murder me." The fire in his eyes warned me to reconsider my words. "Well, you tried to off him. The bigger picture is you coulda sent me to the same place those guys sent my brother. That was sloppy. Now you gotta worry about someone turning your name over to the cops for a five-hundred-dollar tip from crime-stoppers because your crazy ass attempted to kill someone in your own truck," I fumed.

His eyes let me know, I'd hit a nerve even though his facial expression stayed indifferent. "Look, Jazz, I—" he tried to explain, but I'd had enough of listening.

"No, Assata—you look. That's my brother who was buried under all that dirt. Now, I know you're on top of this, but two heads are better than one. I think you'll like my thoughts way better than your methods." I said straddling him and easing down on his readiness. "But, first—tell me everything you've heard about what happened to my brother."

***
~Snow~

Stepping out of the shower, I felt rejuvenated not to mention, I was quarter million dollars richer. My long blonde hair looked almost brunette hanging in a tangled mess down my back. I smiled at the reflection of my perfect D-cups standing proud. Turning around I glanced at my unique ass cheeks. This ass had gotten me into a lot of delicious troubles over the years. It had also gained me some unwanted attention, as well.

Especially, from the hatin' ass sisters that always seemed to find a reason to hate. I wondered, how could they want to whoop my ass simply because their men couldn't control their eyes?

I didn't trip shit like that. I was all about my riches. That's why I never got my heart broken by some worthless ass nigga. I mean, I respected a nigga for what he was worth, but they were all replaceable.

A man turned my life around. He took me from being a high-priced hoe to molding me into a prolific hustler. He had been a beautiful mentor and an even better partner in bed, but his cleverness had become too transparent. Plain and simple I was tired of the bullshit. It's like I was saved from one exploiter, only to be enslaved with another man's selfish fantasy.

That's why even though, it was going to hurt to do it—Bobby had to go. I was meeting him tonight but I was plotting. Before long I would plot his death.

Chapter Nine
Fitting the Pieces

~Ice-Berg~

Me and Nutz sat face to face with the most bread either one of us had ever seen in our young lives as the money machine clicked. My mental was everywhere before bro interrupted my daydreams.

"Damn, nigga—we're ghetto millionaires," he exclaimed. "That's a million and a half in a punk few months. Bro, that ese broad you fuckin' is the truth. You always finding diamonds in the ruff. You need to lace me to where you met her, so I can go snatch me up one." he laughed.

I passed the blunt to him and stood to stretch. "Fam—some shit is better left unspoken. It'll keep us all safe when certain secrets are honored as they're meant to be."

He screwed his face up, "Since when do we keep secrets, bro? Nigga, we blood, and best friends. We don't keep no mu'fuckin'—"

I snatched the Kush stick from his fingers and cut him off. "See, lil' bro, that's the problem with the game. Niggas don't know how to seal their lips. That's what leads to indictments. Benjamin Franklin once wrote, *'The only way to keep a secret between three people is if two of them are dead.'* Now, there's nothing in this world, I wouldn't lace your chucks up to.

"But, I want you to always remember, there's no such thing as no secrets when life and death is on the board. There are some things in life best held close to the chest. The feds can't force outta nigga what he don't know. A goon can't torture the location of the safe from someone who has no idea where it's at. Yet, for the man that risked it all to see my feet back on solid soil. I'll make an exception, but first—I need to know something."

A curious smirk creased my brother's lips. We knew each other so well, he could see the wheels spinning in my head before he spoke. "Fam, fuck you talking too? We came up on the same cornas. Trapped outta tha same projects. I know the game as well as the laws. Yet, what you're forgetting is that we're in the mud together. We know shit about each other, that can get both of us the electric chair. Miss me with the real nigga spill and give it to me straight. No chasa, this yo' shadow you talkin' to, not a worker."

I laughed at my nigga's realism. "We've never kept a secret or fucked each other's bitch. No snake shit in our castle. Kool, folk—sho' you right, but before I tell you the craziest shit you've ever heard. As well as pull you into some shit, that may end up with both of our fuckin' heads busted, let me ask you this." He raised his left eyebrow, quizzically. "You fuckin' that D.A.'s wife, Nutz?"

***

~Destiny~

Everything was set tonight we fully expected my art exhibit would be a smash hit. Me and my friend, Markus who is also the creator of most of these beautiful paintings and sculptures put our all into this night. Sipping from my Martini glass I stared transfixed at the beauty of his work.

"Remarkable, the use of light and shadow—and image that hints at deep pain, yet conveys a promise of hope," I whispered.

"Girl, you've been one of my biggest admirers, and critics since we were in college. Yet, you still find yourself within the contrast. I've known you for most of our adult life. The only time you become so entranced with a color scheme is when your mind is all over the place. So, spill it, bitch." Markus broke through my reverie.

Without taking my eyes away from the painting. I searched for the words to explain my thoughts and feelings.

"Have you ever just wanted to get away from it all? Just pack a bag and leave? Tell nobody where you're going?" Finally, I directed my eyes his way.

As he sipped the yellow concoction in his glass he studied me intently. "Girl, palease, I've been gay for as long as I can remember. Just imagine what I went through being one of three boys, and always attracted to my brother's friends. I've been an outcast my whole life. Of course, I've wanted to just vanish to places where no one knows me. But, Des, that's not how life works. We can't run from ourselves, and we damn sure can't just pack a bag and leave behind things we've invested so much into. Especially, the people who love us regardless of our—shall I say, abnormalities." He struck a pose to make his point.

I laughed at his silliness. "I know that Marky, but when we started this place. Did you ever imagine the success? The failures before it? The stress of it all?"

He narrowed his colorful eyes. "This is about, Sa'Mage, isn't it? You love that man, Des, okay I get that. There's nothing wrong with that. But, you can't allow love to torment you when being in love is the ultimate goal. When was the last time you spoke to him?"

As if on cue the bell above the door chimed alerting us to a new arrival. The person that stepped in caused me to arch my eyebrow but caused Markus to look at me as if to say, "Lucy, you have some explaining to do."

The night would be very interesting, indeed.

***

~Snow~

Ever since Brains introduced me to his sexy ass nephew Assata. I won't lie, the slut in me has been working overtime. I couldn't keep my eyes off his thuggish ass. His girl caught me, eye fucking him a few times the look she gave me, let me know we wouldn't be getting along. Yes, the girl was a bad bitch, to say the least, but I'm no slouch and Snow always gets what she wants. I'm not trying to be wifey or nothin', but I'm gonna fuck him one way or another.

"Bitch, you, betta snap outta whateva has your ass in la la land and focus on what the fuck, I'm saying." Brains seethed.

I focused my attention allowing my eyes to capture every face present. Assata, Jazzy, some dude with funny eyes named Strange, and a pretty boy named Gusto were all present. We all listen intently as Brains bounced his ideas off us. He looked from me to Assata.

"Nephew, this some big boy shit, you and your gal tryna pull off. I dig Jazzy's plan and in a few minutes, shit is gonna get funky. You know, yo' Unk keeps his ears to the street. I have some associates that has a way to kill two birds with one stone. Assata, you just gotta tame that temper of yours, and see beyond the moment. You'll get what you want, but first, let's get to the money."

The expression on Assata's face revealed he was lost. It was amusing to watch as confusion and curiosity stained his hard features. He had no idea how hard it was about to be to tame his temper, once he saw the other piece of Brain's plans.

The sound of the doorbell rang and all eyes went from Brains to the door. Brains smiled at me with a crazed look in his eyes and gestured to the door. I could barely contain my hormones with so much testosterone and 'G' shit in the atmosphere. The bulges under all these niggas shirts told a tale all in itself. I knew this new turn of events was about to set a flame to the fumes in the air. I stood to get the door, but first, I made sure Assata's fine ass was paying attention. I wanted him to see this ass bounce as I strutted away. Just an appetizer to the main course.

***

~Destiny~

Pride surged through me as I observed success in the making. I watched as Markus spoke to a prospective buyer. The man's blue eyes were startling, in contrast to his sun-kissed skin. Curly sandy blonde hair framed his face, taking the edge off the sharp features, that otherwise gave him a dangerous appeal. It's been whispered that the man's money was dirty, but that's none of my business. I'm more interested in the quarter million he intended to spend on merely three pieces of our art collection. Markus worked being two of those pieces. A crowd of nameless, yet important people admired other artwork with the promise of a small fortune by the end of the night.

The champagne in the flute I'd been nursing had become warm, and my nerves were shot. Everyone was oblivious to the darker presence in the room. No one seemed to notice the micro bugs planted all around the room, nor the small lens of the camera's peppered sporadically, well everyone but me and Markus. His posture told me his nerves were as jumpy as

RENTA

mine. I assumed his knowledge of the unsuspected company sprinkled around the room, but most importantly not knowing why they were there.

***

~Ice-Berg ~

The tension was thick as I stood with my hands in the air making it obvious, I was there in peace. This nigga, Assata, and his two road dawgs had they burnas aimed in my direction with deadly intent. The only reason my blood wasn't splashing on the floor, was because this nigga Brains placed himself in the middle of the funk.

Facing his nephew he said. "Assata, you, niggas are being disrespectful. Put the shit up and sit down. If you ain't feeling the spill the nigga gives, y'all can whack the nigga at your own discretion. But, if one drop of blood touches my Persian carpet, you, niggas won't be too far behind him."

He then looked at me. "Young, nigga, I came up with your ole man back in the day. He did me a few solids when I needed a helping hand. Since them, white folks has him locked away in their prison. I've been repaying my debt by helping you reach your goals, but you and my nephew got blood in y'all eyes that I won't stand in the middle of. So, for the sake of everyone involved make this nigga see why it's in the best interest of us all to place the bullshit on hold."

I looked to Assata. He was the only one that still had his banger on display. His eyes were on fire and there was no time to waste. He honestly didn't give a fuck about his uncle's Persian rug.

***

~Nutz~

"Damn—I can't see how niggas be wearing this typa shit?" I was fresh to death fa sho', but the tuxedo jacket was way too fitted for a nigga of my stature. Fuck it—I'm out here. There was a cluster of uptight looking ass niggas standing around conversing about God knows what. They must've thought I couldn't hear because the dialogue became hushed as I passed. Something made me glance at the person nearest me, and a moment of craziness surged through me. I could've sworn, I'd seen the sucka somewhere before. I almost stopped to ask him, but the mission I was on caused me to keep it moving. Yet, I couldn't shake the sick feeling eating at a nigga.

"Damn—I'm trippin' but I never forgot a face. There ain't too many niggas, that a nigga will confuse for a District Attorney," I told myself.

A quick glance back assured me that I was trippin', or was I? The Kush had me on one even though it wasn't him. I coulda sworn, I saw six people when I passed now there was only five. No more Kush for the boy tonight.

***

~ Assata~

"Man, you mu'fuckas gotta be stupid or summin' Unk. I can't believe you even entertaining this shit. Nigga, this a suicide mission." I was burning up as I paced a hole in my uncle's floor.

The whole room had their eyes on me. I looked to Jazzy her eyes were down, and that sexy ass look she gets when deep in thought was evident.

"I know you ain't considering this shit, Jazz?"

Her hazel-greens raised and focused on me. "Assata, baby, the nigga explained his plan of action. If I must say so myself it's a pretty good one. I think we can pull it off G, but shit like this will take all of us under one umbrella. I know you—"

"Fuck that shit you talkin' 'bout." I dead that shit she was bumpin'. "These pussy ass niggas smoked yo' blood, and you wanna trust them with our lives?" I turned my wrath on my flesh and blood. "Unk, you know, you've been like a pops to me, but you outta line bringing my enemy here. This ain't how it—" my words caught in my throat as the white girl, Snow strutted into the room.

Her hair was pulled back into a tight bun and the strapless, white, Versace dress she was squeezed into molested her curves. She gave Unk a brief glance setting her sights on me.

"Assata, I know, it's not my place to speak on your business, but this is the problem with men. Y'all allow pride to guide your footsteps. Then by the time, it's too late to react, all that can be said is, "I fucked up." But, 'I fucked up means nothing when you've sacrificed your whole camp on a whim, or missed out on millions because your insight couldn't surpass your hindsight. I've been involved with some made men in my life, every one of them fell victim to their own arrogance. My advice is that you place your beef to the side if only for a moment and get this money. I can't tell you if these other men are trustworthy or not. But, I can tell you that this pussy comes with a money back guarantee if it doesn't serve its purpose."

The look in her eyes hinted at her double meaning, but I'm not a tender dick nigga. I don't give a fuck 'bout none of that shit.

"Look, I'm sure you may be able to pull it off, but the fact still remains this sucka right here had a hand in my right hand's death and I want—" before I could finish my sentence.

I was face to face with the deadly side of a bad mu'fucka, with a clip so long I wondered how I'd missed it from the jump.

"Look, Assata, we've been at it since lil' niggas. I've slumped some of yours and you put even more of mine in the dirt. You know, I don't fear you and you know without a shadow of a doubt, that my pistol bust just like yours. I'ma say this one time and never say it again—" the nigga stared into my eyes without blinking. "I didn't eighty-six that nigga, Shy. You think I'd put yo' ace in the dirt nigga, and be stupid enough to trust you at my back in a plot to get cake? Assata, you know, we cut from the same cloth. I'm here to break bread with you and yo' circle not fuck over you."

The nigga's eyes never left mine, even though he had to hear the distinctive sounds of slugs being jacked into the chambers of Gusto and Strange's burnas.

"We can end this shit right now, fam. Yea, yo' squad can shut my lights out, but I doubt either one's aim is precise enough to do so before I do you. The thing is if we get this shit jumping we all lose. You'll die without knowing the nigga that smoked yo' boy. I'll die without being able to spend the loot I've risked it all for, and we'll both miss the opportunity of a lifetime."

With that being said the nigga took the tool outta my face and stepped back. I smiled and with the quickness of a viper, I went straight in his mu'fuckin' mouth and dropped him to his back pockets.

"Nigga, you bet not ever pull a tool on me, and not use it." I hissed before Jazzy stepped between us.

"Assata stop this is dumb shit, bae," she screamed as her eyes filled with water. "I know you got blood in your eyes, hell we all know that. But, baby, Shy's gone and no matter how much blood you taint these streets with, he—he's not coming back, A." Her eyes pleaded with me as murder danced in mine.

Something in her gaze spoke to me in a language only we could comprehend. "She's right nigga—let's get this bread. After we fill the safe we can fill a tub up with the blood of, Shy's killa." Gusto said beside me before he looked to Berg. "I've never fucked with yo' side for the sake of you, and everybody you're close to. I hope you ain't had a hand in my nigga's death." He then looked to Strange. "I'm in, fam."

Slowly, but surely nods of agreement went around the room until the only ones left on the outside of the plan was me and Jazzy.

"I'm with you wrong or right. If you with it, I'm with it—if you ain't feeling it we can walk out this door, right now."

She let it be known where her loyalties stood. My eyes were burning into Berg.

"This Russian nigga is about that action, fam. I've been plotting on the sucka for a minute and can't see how to get at the boy. He's plugged in with some heavy mu'fuckas and he ain't no slouch."

"So, tell me again, how we gonna get the ups on this pussy boy?" Brains slapped me on the back.

"Well, Neph, that's where your uncle comes into play," he said smiling at Snow.

"Baby girl you know what to do."

***

~Destiny~

"Boy stop," I gushed as Nutz stood behind me with his arm securely around my waist.

He'd sucked my neck so many times, I wouldn't have been surprised if there was a mark of passion there.

"So, baby, is that him?" I whispered.

Nutz tensed as he pulled me even closer to him. "Shush," he demanded with a stern face. "Watch your mouth, Des— that's not your business. Damn, I don't even know why I told you the business," he fumed.

I turn to him and wrap my arms around his neck. "Baby, I'm sorry. I wasn't being nosey or nothing. I've just never been a part of anything like this. I want you to know I'm down that's all." I put on a small pout for him.

As he kissed my lips I could tell he was over it just that fast. "It's Gucci, ma just walk light, so you won't piss the ground off," he replied before looking at his watch. "Where the fuck is she?" He whispered more to himself than to me.

As if on cue one of the most gorgeous creatures that even I'd ever set eyes on walked into my establishment. Jealousy kissed me internally as I watched a strange smile blossom from Nutz lips.

"So, you got jungle fever now, handsome?" I joked.

He took his eyes off her for a fraction of a moment, only to say something that left me speechless. "Ma, I've never fucked a white girl before in my life, but this bitch even has your pussy wet. Would you fuck her?"

My silence encouraged him.

"I thought so," he smiled. "It's not jungle fever the bitch just got that effect on people—niggas and bitches alike.

***

~Snow~

I strutted into the gallery as if I was poetry in motion. I stood in the middle of the room allowing my eyes to scan the floor, but the disappointment that eased into my expression revealed to all who had eyes to see, I'd been stood up. Turning my sights on a portrait of a nude woman crying by a river. I strutted over to it and studied its beauty like an avid fan. The title of it is was *'Cry me a River'* the allure of it had actually taken my breath away.

"Beautiful, isn't it?" A masculine voice made love to my ears from behind me.

I knew who it was without turning around. Only a powerful man treasured the notion of 'why waste time'.

"I think it's powerful—the standard of true beauty," I replied.

Turning to face him I found myself swimming in the depths of his piercing eyes. I had never really been attracted to white boys but that turned me on. He could get this pussy with no fight.

I slowly licked my lips and accepted the flute of wine he handed me.

"Yes," he smiled. "Yes, it's a beauty, but it pales in contrast to the masterpiece standing before me. Your name is?" His accent was heavy Middle Eastern, maybe.

I took his outstretched hand and as he pulled mine to his lips I smiled.

"Tiffany, but you can call me Tiff, and you are?" He never took his eyes away from mine, as he began to scare the hell out of me.

"Lucifer—me and the devil have the same name—nice to meet you, Tiff."

***

~**Detective Hunter**~

"So, tell me again, why we've bugged this funky little art gallery?" I questioned the man whose name I won't mention, just yet. He along with my partner Winslet, a few D.E.A boys, and I sat in the back of a utility van watching history be made. The respectable establishment had become a den of snakes. Not only did we have international drug smuggler, Obolensky a.k.a Russia but also the Bureau's favorite girl, Snow all in the same room.

The icing on the cake was not the simple fact that they were being introduced, but more of how and why they'd come to be in acquaintance. The street punk Nutz was as smart as he was stupid. He'd literally talked his way into a federal indictment. The man that set this investigation in motion sat beside me.

"We've bugged this place because this is where it begins. As we speak there are two other team of agents in other locations monitoring the other piece of this enigma. This is bigger than you think detective. We've chased Bobby Ray a.k.a Brains and his exploits all over the world. Only to find him in his last phase of work. If it wasn't for the superior work of my informant, that I will not mention Mr. Brains would be thought to be retired, but not only have we caught back up to his trail. We can be certain he's elevated his status as an international con man. To a conspirator to commit murder, as well as linking us to one of the most prolific drug operations the U.S. has seen since Big Meech and his B.M.F stories. We're in alliance with the A.T.F and your division. This time David Swanson, is going down and he's bringing company." he declared.

I smiled and patted him on the back.

"Says the man that's made a mockery of the Federal Government for your sake let's hope you're right."

Chapter Ten
Blood—Camera—Action

~Snow~

Four weeks had passed since my introduction to the king-pin, Russia. He'd done almost everything in his power to spoil me, outside of buying me the drop head Rolls Royce, I hinted at wanting for my birthday. It still amazed me how powerful a man could be, until his dick was wet, and his nuts were empty. I'd only known the man for a short while, and in his attempt to try to impress me he'd revealed so much. I knew that he kept a portion of his shipments at a warehouse in a small town outside of Dallas called Desoto.

He sends a quarter of that to a two-story house on the out-skirts of here and allows his youngest brother to lead the street operations. As well as have whatever he needed in terms of weight on standby when needed. I tell you being a white girl with ass had its perks. He spent more time with me than he did with his own wife. She must be one of those out of shape bor-ing women because her man's craving for this pussy was pri-mal.

I've yet to give in, but I've sucked his cock until he was at the brink of eruption. However, I always stop before he nuts. Being a seductress takes more than having a pretty face and nice body. It's levels to this shit and I'm on the top floor. At the moment, I was surrounded by two beautiful women. We were inside this plush stretch limousine Jazzy, me, and a long-legged Mexican chick Brains implemented into our mission. We were sitting and enjoying shots of Pure Hennessy White.

The drive to our destination had been filled with laughter. Even though, it was just us women. I could see that Jazzy was a really cool chick. Yes, I'm still gonna fuck her dude, but she is a real bitch, and I'd never been the type to speak against another woman. My attraction to Assata wouldn't allow me to consider her a friend, but if only for tonight we were cool as a breeze. As I gazed out of the tinted windows, I noticed the landscape had changed. We pulled up to the two-story house and this mofo was beautiful.

A medicated lawn equipped with a snaking driveway complimented the red brick structure. We'd met here a few times before because he said it was convenient. I figured it was the last place his wife would suspect him to be with another bitch. Risky, but crafty. I watched as the driver stepped out and searched for weapons. I assumed the two guards were satisfied because they allowed him to step away over to our door.

I smiled and stepped out with grace. Jazzy and the Mexican chick I'd come to know as Mya followed my lead. If I must say so myself the three of us together created a picture of perfection. The red Christian Dior cocktail dress, I wore set off the four-inch heels that laced up my calves and stopped with an exotic bow behind my knees. My hair flowed down my back.

Jazzy and Mya were no less beautiful in similar dresses by Oscar De la Renta. Even the guards seem awestruck. They were so lost in their lust for beauty, they led us to their boss without searching us. Mya openly admired the cottage style structure.

"Now, this shit is sexy, mamis. Wait that's not the word I'm looking for," she frowned slightly before looking to Jazzy. They burst out laughing the cognac was working its magic. Before pulling off our driver honked his goodbyes. We all waved.

***

~Assata~

I pulled the limo over a few blocks from the house. Screwing the suppressor onto the semi-automatic, I summoned the beast within me. I didn't know how this shit was gonna spin, but it was either go hard or go home. The 'G' in me wasn't hearing none of that go home shit. Stepping outta the car I glanced around to make sure no eyes were on me. The earpiece in my ear crackled to life.

"Nephew, it's all on you now. The ladies are in but two guards are outside the door. Remember what I told you," Brains said.

I frowned, I musta missed whatever part of the conversation he was referring to.

"Unk, fuck you talm-bout, what you told me?" I questioned.

The silly ass old man burst out laughing. "Nigga, I know, I ain't no pimp but pimp remember what I told you," he laughed.

I joined in on the laughter as I foot back to where I'd just dropped my bitch off. I hoped she was tougher than Six when it came down to it 'cause I was about to put my gangsta shit down.

***

~The Squad~

Brains, Nutz, Berg, Strange, and Gusto awaited the signal, that would let them know it was show time. The black Envoy they were in was so cloudy with smoke. It was hard to see one's hand if he put it in someone's face. What was distinctive, was the sound of clips being checked, and slugs being jacked into place. Every weapon involved had clips that held thirty or more bullets. Every nigga there had put their murder game down at one point or another.

Nutz was the first to break the silence. "Say, Berg, you know I love you, right?"

Not sure if he was showing a sign of weakness all eyes turn to him. "Nigga fuck you on—you catching pussy or something?" Gusto spat.

Nutz ignored him. "Do you, nigga?" He repeated to his brother.

"Nutz, you, my mu'fuckin', brother. You know, I love you, nigga. If you spooked though you can switch places with me and be the driver. I'll go in and put my murder one down. You know I'm—"

"Man shut the fuck up, cuz. You as well as these monkey ass niggas right here know I'm 'bout this life. You also know you can't go in there just in case shit don't turn out right."

"I asked you what I asked cause you trust these niggas with our lives. If they get the double cross in the mix for us. When we get to hell I'ma make sure I hit you dead in yo' mu'fuckin mouth." The whole truck exploded in laughter, well, everyone except Nutz and Gusto.

Even through the fog of smoke, the twinkle of Gusto's gold teeth could be seen being an evil sneer.

***

~ Assata~

As I made my way up the driveway, I saw the two guards that searched me when I dropped the girls off. The one closest to me stiffened upon seeing me. I raised my hands in the air to show him, that I was unarmed. I hated the tight ass suit Brains forced me to wear. The Glock .40 in the small of my back was digging in my skin with each step. I stopped about eight feet away from them. Their hands tightened on the Mac 11's they had on full display. The dark shades hid their eyes, I knew they were watching for the slightest reason to air my black ass out, but my posture was free of malice or drama.

The big mu'fucka said, "No te acerques mas."

The look on my face must have told them, I didn't comprehend whatever the fuck he'd just said. Cause the second nigga spoke in English.

"Don't come any closer—" he paused "Where you car limo man?"

With my hands still in the air, I gave him my spiel. "Look, I'm not trying to disturb you boys. I just caught a flat 'bout a block away, and I ain't got no car jack to change the tire. I was just—"

The shorter dude said something in Spanish, that musta been funny and disarming because they laughed, and the tension in their bodies relaxed.

"We no care about you problem, senor. You need to leave this place until you are called. Tis ting you speak of is you own dilemma"

Heat began to surge through me. '*Pussy ass ese tryin' to flex on me 'cause he knows I'm outgunned*'. I turned my eyes to big boy. He showed his spite by spitting on the ground by my feet. I noticed his hand tap the butt of his heat. I looked from the glob of spit back to the muscle faced sucka. I smiled, nodded, and turned to walk away.

"One more thing before I go," I said through clenched teeth.

I spun back in their direction yanking the tool from its resting spot. The temperature changed as I hit big boy first. I didn't need too much aim the extend on my burner was my assurance. I just squeezed with thirty bullets in the extendo, I was assured to hit something. Big Boy's face exploded as his glasses flew up in the air. Silent kisses of fire slipped from the bidness side of the .40.

I walked to the beef rather than tryin' to duck and dodge. I saw the last nigga standing trying to shake his surprise. I whacked his stupid ass for nutting up when the beef was on. Two to the chest dropped homie before he could get a grip on the Mac. He wheezed and clutched his chest as if he could stop his life from slipping away from him. I stood over him and put the burna to his face. His breath was ragged, and his eyes pleaded with me.

"Maybe you will be more respectful in yo' next life," I growled giving him two to the face.

Tapping the earpiece I sent the signal to the wolves. Just for good measure, I picked up lil' man's Mac 11.

My earpiece crackled, "We're bending the kona, fam." Gusto's voice came through.

I looked around at all the mess I'd caused with little sound. I gotta find out where Unk got these suppressors from.

***

~Jazzy~

All eyes were on me as I put on the show of my lifetime. I'd never been a stripper, but tonight I was all the way out of my body. Sensually, I rolled my belly to the melody of *'Beyoncé's 'Strip for You'* playing from my iPhone. I watched Mya deep throat Solomon. Solomon is Russia's brother. He had boyish features with his brother's eyes. He seemed real mellow especially in comparison to his older brother. Who seemed to exude an air of danger and mischief.

Not long after we arrived him and Snow disappeared up the stairs leaving me and Mya, with Solomon and two other foreigners. I honestly couldn't distinguish the ethnicity of. What I did know was after a few drinks. Which I assumed was spiked, because I'd only sipped a little. My senses were way too sharp not to mention, my hormones were on fire for no apparent reason shit had gotten a little wild.

Mya wasted no time with the two she'd all but manhandled. As she sucked one dry, the other was behind her sweating like a slave and knocking the lining out of her poor little coochie. The third man sat on the couch opposite of them stroking himself into a frenzy, watching me squeeze my nipples.

"Lord, please let Assata, hurry up," I whispered to myself smiling for pretense.

As if God was laughing at my request mister small dick jumped up and headed my way with his little worm in his hands. I put my palm against my chest stopping him short.

"Hold up lover boy." The look of confusion on his face was priceless. "Patience makes the pussy wetter." I murmured and took his manhood into my hands, guiding him back to the couch. Pulling his face to my nipples I sighed as I stroked him. Baby needed to hurry the fuck up. I was nothing like Snow and Mya. I'd fuck around and get us all killed, because I ain't fucking, sucking, or even taking off my panties. That's on Shy's grave.

***

~ Assata~

Soon as the squad walked up the driveway and saw my work. My nigga Gusto showed all thirty-two of the gold fronts in his mouth. Even from behind the ski-mask I could see thirst for blood surging through him.

"I woulda gave em' the whole clip all face shots." He whispered in my ear. "But, nice work champ."

I smiled pulling the ski-mask out of my back pocket. I pull it over my face, then put my finger to my lips, and demanded silence. As I twisted the doorknob I could only pray that it wasn't locked. The galaxies must have been on my side, because not only was it unlocked it opened without sound.

***

~**Jazzy**~

Shit done got real. I don't rock like this at all, but with this nympho bitch Mya taking it in every orifice she had. The cat I was entertaining was animalistic with lust. So, I had to choose between the lesser of three evils. It was either give him head, let him fuck, or let him suck my pussy. The first two would be blaspheme, so I let the nigga pull my panties to the side and lick this pussy. He was doing his thing. Unconsciously, I gripped the back of his head. I decided I may as well get a nut before the fireworks begin.

Well, at least that was my plan until I looked up from this pussy eating ass foreigner, sucking my kitty, and set sights on eight pairs of evil eyes boring into the freak show on public display. Being as though his back was to the door, he didn't see the nightmare behind him.

I cleared my throat. "Umm, I don't think our company is satisfied with y'all's performance." I assumed that my lack of participation caused the look of confusion on his face, or maybe it was the statement I'd just made. Whichever it was he sat up on his knees and attempted to glance backward. What happened next transpired in slow motion.

A mixture of grayish matter and thick blood, sprayed stains on my pussy and stomach as his face exploded. As he fell face forward, I got a glimpse of the socket where his right eye used to be. Frantically, I shoved him off me and tried to wipe his brain matter and blood off my skin, but it only seemed to lather like I was putting on lotion.

Maybe I was in shock or on my way to it because a small shrill scream came from deep within me. I honestly didn't know how, because my mouth seemed to be locked shut.

"Shut that hoe up, fam," Assata growled.

Gusto moved in my direction with a monstrous gun in his hand. *'It's over with',* I thought. I threw my hands out in front of me as if I could block a bullet from piercing my flesh. To my surprise and horror, two gentle coughs from his pistol quieted the room and sent me to an early grave. Then everything went black.

***

~Nutz~

I smirked at these boy's work. The Mexican bitch was slumped over the couch with two in her chest. Bitch was bad too. Silly hoe shouldn't have been doing all that screaming! Just a waste of pussy. I saw Gusto's aim was getting better, though.

"Oh shit, Jazz," Me and Assata said in unison.

We rushed to her. I was thinking why the fuck did he involve her, anyway? That shit made me wanna whack his bitch ass. Jazzy, ain't the typa bitch, that needs to be a part of this kinda shit. Now, look she done passed the fuck out from the slightest sight of blood. Movement out the corner of my eyes made me swing the tool in that direction.

Strange had the two eses or whatever the fuck they were on their knees. They looked pathetic with shriveled up dicks, and sweat pouring from their session with Mya. They must've been immune to death because they kept it 'G' under our get down. Well, one of them the other nigga looked like he was 'bout to piss himself. I assumed he wasn't tryna face the same fate as his boy because the pussy spoke up.

"I'm Russia's cousin, me show you where the money and coca is if you let me live." He said with a heavy accent.

I looked to Assata he looked at the man in his eyes and vowed to let him breathe if he made our jobs easier. The cat glanced over to his homie, but the slim baby face mu'fucka glared at him shaking his head. He said something in whatever language they speak. They had the nuts to glare back at us as if there was a reward for being brave. I respected the lion though. At least he would die with dignity.

"The coke is in the kitchen underneath the refrigerator. All you do is remove the vegetable tray at the bottom. You'll see that it opens up to a hole in the floor. You'll find what you are looking for." The lamb of the two explained.

Assata looked to Brains and Strange without words they headed to see 'bout homies claims.

"The money?" I questioned.

He looked from Assata to me before he replied. "It's in the safe behind the portrait of the Chateau de Villandry. The code is—" The stubborn one hit him with a right cross before Assata shot him in his side.

He crumbled as he clutched his wound. The mu'fucka must've been crazy because a wicked smile touched his lips as he whispered. "Ye' gonna visit de devils when Russia sees ye treachery."

By now Jazzy had come around and Assata said to me. "Say dawg get her out of here."

Instinctively, I frowned at the nigga. He may run these other niggas but he had me fucked up. I was 'bout to tell him just that until, Jazzy stepped to me taking my hand. Her eyes were lost. I knew this wasn't the time to be on no freak shit. Her nipples stood at attention and the speckles of blood staining them made my dick hard, maybe I really am a nut case.

***

~Assata~

I stood behind the homie as he opened the safe. As it swung open stacks on top of stacks of big faces stared back at me.

"Turn around slowly, homie. Don't do nothing that'll make me paint all that bread with your last thoughts."

Folk turned around sweat made his face look almost comical, as he stared at me with the million-dollar question in his eyes.

"Me give you what you come for you gave your word not to—to kill me." he stammered.

A hint of my diamonds pecked from behind my lips. "My word is solid, fam. I'm not going to kill you."

His body relaxed as he smiled in relief. "Thank you! Thank you. You won't regret it, I—"

The smile slipped from my lips as I shut him down. "Naw dawg I never said you wasn't' going to die. I just said I wasn't going to kill you."

Panic tainted his facial. "But—but you said—" that's all that escaped his lips before hollows rocked him to sleep eternally.

"Your cowardness killed you pussy! In the next life be a gangsta." I hissed at his corpse as I gave him three more to the body, just cause he was a pussy. I looked up at all this bread. "Damn!" This was the true definition of blood money!

I laughed, then a sound behind me made me spin with the tool ready to bark.

"Whoa, lil' daddy, be careful with that thing!" My uncle said dropping a bag at my feet. "Twenty bricks—uncut—stamp is fresh looks like dude was connected with the Cartel." He looked around. "Where's Snow, Neph?"

***

~Brains~

We left Strange to bag up the money and wait for our return. As I climbed the stairs behind my nephew my heart beat against my chest. I'm getting too old for this shit. Me and Assata crept up the stairs with our pistols raised and ready to fire. The silence was thick. There was too many closed doors where a mu'fucka could hide. I won't lie I was nervous. I'm not no killa I pay niggas to solve problems. I'm not no new jack but this ain't my vibe. Assata stopped suddenly making me run into him. He glared back at me as I was the cause.

He pointed to the room on the left wing and back at himself, then to the right indicating he was going that way. This son of a bitch was trying to split up. Without waiting for my response, he took off leaving me no other choice, but to follow instructions. A sick feeling caused acid to rush up my throat but I forced it down. Stepping to my bidness I put my ear to the closed door, silence. I eased the door open, heart pounding, and gun leading the way like I'd seen in the movies.

Relief flooded through me empty. I turned to go to the next room, but the sight of my nephew standing in the doorway straight ahead stopped me short. It wasn't that he was just standing there staring. It wasn't even that his body language spoke a million words that caused tears to flood my vision. It was more of the fact, that he wasn't pointing his gun like they do in the movies.

***

~ Assata~

I'd found Snow she was laying naked on silk sheets with blood flowing from her like a fountain. A window in the corner was open and the drapes blew in the wind. Shit was 'bout to get ugly, fam. The mission was to whack the Russian and rob him, but the moment called for other shit. Uncle B shoved me out of the way and stepped into the room. Seeing his bitch with her throat slit fucked him up. He cried but no tears fell.

"Unk, we gotta get the fuck outta here. That Russian mu'fucka got away, ain't no telling how he's rocking right now." I looked over at Snow he leaned over her and just stared. "Unk, we gotta—go." I hissed losing patience.

He closed her eyes and without looking at me, he headed for the door. That's when all hell broke loose and gunshots sounded off below us. We looked at each other and rushed out the door. Maybe the nigga was in shock, or his intentions was to just join his bitch. Before I could stop him my uncle ran down the flight of stairs. Even though I was only a few feet behind him I couldn't stop him from his intentions.

I watched as he hit the last step with his tool spitting in the direction of the living room. Don't ask me how the nigga knew where to find trouble. I don't know, but what I did know was

149

he found exactly what he was looking for. I watched him shoot it out slug for slug, with whomever he was having a drawdown with. His body jerked a few times but the way he worked lead me to think he was safe.

I ran the rest of the way down the stairs swinging the burna in the direction Unk was aiming. Only to find nothing there. Blood was everywhere. Cautiously, I walked deeper into the room. Instantly pain, anger, and regret ate at me. Strange was D.O.A, looking over at what musta happened, my heart hurt for my dawg. The bitch ass Russian I hit in his side musta still been amongst the living. He waited us out, mayne!

The bullshit high point .380 that laid on the floor beside him, told me our mistake of not being more observant.

"Let's get this shit and murk out Unk—shit not right," I said as I begin picking up stacks that musta fell out the trash bags that came from God knows where.

"Unk, snap out of that shit and let's get this shit ova wit," I snapped.

Turning to see what his fucking problem was my heart shut down. "Naw, come on Bobby Ray," I broke as I rushed over to my flesh.

He was leaking with his back against the wall. A blood-red smear ran down the wall as he musta used it to slide down. Tears tainted my vision.

"Damn Unk," I looked down at the holes in his chest. "Fuck," I screamed as I punched a hole in the wall. "See God this why I lose faith," I whispered to the wind.

Brains coughed up blood then smiled at me. "Did—did I—did I get him, ne—neph?"

I just nodded as rain stormed down my face.

"Assata, we got to—" Nutz began as he entered with his burna clutched.

He observed the massacre all around us. We locked eyes and my vibration was intense. He walked over to the bags and started snatching shit up.

"Fam, them people on the way—we gotta burn." He mumbled as he heaved two bags over his shoulders.

I looked back at Unk he'd already crossed over on me.

"Send my love to my T-lady and squad old man. I'll catch up when it's my time." I saluted as I did to him what he did to Snow. I closed fam eyes so he wouldn't see the madness suffocating a nigga.

Chapter Eleven
Love and Betrayal

~Six~

It had been three months since the shit went down with the New York, nigga. Even now, I couldn't believe, I walked away with my life. Me and Assata haven't really been vibing like we used to. Maybe he was still fucked up about me freaking out on him. I'm merely a woman. I love that nigga to death and will go to the ends of the earth for him, but I'm no killer. I miss my boo, though. I've called him too many times in the past week.

I'd even reached out to his boy Gusto, but something wasn't right about him. He'd called me a few times and seemed cool, but I refrained from talking to him too much, so he wouldn't get the wrong impression. Thinking about Assata was crazy. I'd only seen him three times since the situation, neither time had he fucked me. I even went as far as—

My phone started ringing, speaking of the devil. A big smile graced my lips when I heard *'One Plus One'* by *Beyoncé*. It's the ringtone I had for Assata.

"Heeeyyy baby," I gushed. This nigga brought the woman out of me.

"I'm pulling up step outside, mama," he said before the call dropped.

My smile slipped. Looking at the screen, I realized this nigga was on some bullshit. The bass from this nigga's whip was so loud it vibrated my window. His favorite song, *'Always Be'* by *MO3* made me smile. This nigga listened to that song at least a thousand times and still fuck with it like it's his first time.

I rushed to slide into a pair of forces. The boy shorts and muscle shirt, I was wearing was enough to entice any nigga even though it was loungewear. All this ass and thighs I had even a nigga of Assata's pedigree couldn't resist. The day was sunny as I stepped outside. From my second story apartment, I could see the glare of his jewels as he sat on the hood of his Chevy SS. Like always the nigga had generated the attention of all the ladies.

Shayla a petite chocolate girl, that stayed on the first floor was always up in his face. Even though Assata wasn't officially my nigga, these hoes 'round here knew the deal. Soon as she saw me, she put on this fake ass smile, as if she wouldn't slice my throat the moment I turned my back.

"Heeyy, girl, I was just telling Assata how hot this burgundy paint job is," the bitch lied.

I rolled my eyes at her, before narrowing my eyes at his black ass. He had this little gesture he always did with his left eyebrow when he was amused.

"What's good, ma. I ain't did nothin'. You know, I wouldn't disrespect the game like that, but if you consider lil' mama right here yo' potna. You need to find a better choice of friends." His bluntness seemed to rattle her because her eyes bucked, and she looked as if she couldn't believe he'd just put her on blast.

He hopped off the hood and headed for the driver's side. Before sliding behind the wheel, he looked over to me and said, "You gonna stand there looking stupid? Or you gonna get in and at least act like you didn't just insult me?" He looked over to Shayla. "I woulda respect you more if you woulda just kept it funky with her and told her you wanna fuck me. I'm the God of my universe—she's my rida, but not my bitch. You'll get further by keepin' it one-hundred, ma. Stay up.

***

~Jazzy~

The woman sitting across from me was only a shell of her former self. The last time I saw Keisha she was vibrant and happily in love with my brother. Even though, it had been a few years since we'd seen each other. It was crazy to see the effects time, and the lack of self-worth could have on a person. This woman used to be one of the prettiest women in my neighborhood. The envy of her time, yet this creature sitting before me contradicted my claim, as she tried to finger comb her dry hair.

The bags under her eyes aged her terribly and her skin was so taut, her bones seem to be a second away from poking through. Her skin was so splotchy and it was just pitiful to see the aftermath of a fallen star.

"Why the fuck do you keep looking at me like that?" She growled I could see shame all over her face like a shadow.

"Kesh, you can't keep living like this," I said as I waved my hand around the living room littered with takeout containers.

The floor hadn't been vacuumed and the smell of stale cigarettes hung in the air. "This shit ain't you at all girl, we're boss bitches. Remember you once told me, that the difference between a bitch and a boss bitch was the attitude and morale? Kesh, we're all fucked up about, Shy but—"

"Jazz, you don't know what it's like to live like this. Shy was—is my soulmate. I can't close my eyes without seeing—" water streamed down her face and she breathed deeply. "He's my every thought, Jazz. I can't fuck with another man without feeling nasty. I—I—"

I watched as the rest of her strength slipped and she folded over, with her face in her hands. The sister in me caused me to walk over and hold her as tight as I could. It's a powerful thing, emotions.

"When it's real—the love, when the love is solid, you feel that shit!" I sympathize with this queen, my heart spilled from my eyes in the form of liquid. "It has to pass, Kesh—he would want you to live, baby girl. He would want you to be—" her sudden actions stopped me short.

She sat up straight with resolution. With hot tears running down her face, she fucked my world all the way up. "No, you don't understand, Jazzy. I'm tired—I'm sooo tired." she moaned.

My confusion at her sudden change of expression must have been all over my face because she cupped my face in her hands. "Jazzy, you have to get Shy's phone. The last person he talked to was the one who killed him. I heard the whole conversation."

***

~ Assata~

I had shorty at the lake in Lake Dallas. It was warm out and the best part 'bout it was, that outside of a couple further up shore it was just us. Lil' Baby sat with her knees pulled close to her chest, as she stared out at the waves of the water rolling onto the sand by our feet. The wind blew softly, carrying the aroma of this gas, that I was trying my best not to choke on down the shore. My eyes rolled over her lil' thick ass. The boy shorts couldn't hold all that ass, so it escaped from the bottom forcing the back of 'em up her ass crack.

I don't know if she'd done that shit on purpose, or if she just didn't feel it. Naw, she did that shit on purpose, but I'll play along.

"Say, yo' shit hungry?" I asked.

She looked at me with a frown. "Naw, I'm good, I ate before you showed up." I smiled, this shit was too easy. "So, why yo' ass snackin' on them shorts like that?" I busted out laughing.

She tried to play tough, but that shit didn't last as she took a playful swing at me. "Shut up, boy!"

Somehow, we ended up wrestling, and in the end, she was on top of me. Yeah, that shit was purposely! Sand was all over her arms and chest. I assumed the cool breeze, was what had her chocolate nipples peeking through the muscle tee. This shit was gonna be hard, but lil' one is my baby, and she deserved the real. I sat up with her still in my lap, face to face like a real nigga 'pose to be, with a solid bitch and opened my chest to my queen.

"Do you believe in destiny, Six? I ain't talking 'bout that shit them white people be talm-bout in the movies. I'm talking 'bout that real deep shit. That, yeahhh, this what it's all about typa shit?"

She searched my eyes for an indication, why I was asking her this typa shit. "Do I believe that God has a plan for us—" she began.

I placed my fingers to her lips. "Naw, queen, I respect the O.G. I honestly don't know if he exists or not, but I've been barking at dawg my whole life, still I'm waiting for answers. That's not what I mean. See, baby girl, when people are unsure of shit, or can't explain certain aspects of life they use God as a rationality. Only God knows, or if it's God's plan—but God does know." I brushed sand off the side of her face, as my eyes study hers intently. "Just because a baby comes out of the womb stillborn, or an innocent little girl gets hit by a stray bullet in a chaotic situation, doesn't mean it was in God's plan." I don't know what made me do it, but my hands took on a mind of their own, as they traveled over her body. I smoothed them down her back, over her ass cheeks, and down her thighs, then finally rested them on her waist.

"That shit was a sign, that the devil is just as real as the O.G. The negative to the positive of life. No way to have one without the other." Six wrapped her arm around my neck, maybe my touch was misleading. But, this might have been the last time, I'd get to explore her touch, so I did nothing to discourage it. I told her to stand up and with a look of confusion, she obliged.

Still confused she reached out her hand and helped me to my feet. Hand in hand, I lead her down to the shore, witnessing the beauty of the horizon. "Destiny is the magnification of one's creation. If God is up there, he allows us to create destiny. That's why in your Bible it says, *faith without work is dead*! If a mu'fucka believes in something, you work to make that dream a reality. We are controllers of where we end up." Six released my hand and folded her arms like she could read my mind and knew exactly where the conversation was headed.

"Yeah, sometimes shit don't turn out as we plan, but that's what works. It's that faith in you to see the end of shit. Destiny is where we end up, feel me, ma?" I looked over in her direction.

She bit her bottom lip and nodded her head. "Six, you're my nigga. We've been thuggin' for a minute, I've always kept it 'G' with you."

Without blinking I came from the hip with mama. "I've met—well—I've known her for a while and we talkin' 'bout rockin'. We not official and I'd never cast you to the side, but lil' mama got a piece of my heart. A long time ago, I made a promise to a nigga I love dearly, and –" she shut me up by putting her hand over my mouth.

"So, it's true?" she whispered.

"Huh, is what true?"

Tears clouded her eyes and without another word, Six took off running.

"Damn, Shy, I'm trying to do this shit right, dawg," I whispered, before getting up following, Ms. Lady.

***

~**Jazzy**~

I'd been calling Assata's ass for hours. As I sped through traffic, I couldn't focus. Kesha told me the whole conversation, she'd overheard Shy having. She told me, that she begged him not to go but just like so many niggas before him, he overestimated a woman's intuition. The thing eating at me the most, was how she said Shy ended the call. There are only four niggas that use that code and know the meaning of it. Assata's phone was still going to voicemail, as I pulled up to my mama's house.

It was as run down as ever and as I stared at the poverty surrounding me. All I could do was thank God for being my Father. Anxiety consumed me as I pressed the call button for the third time. '*Why does Assata have his phone off?*'

Frustration surged through me until a light came on in my head. Gusto would know what's up with, 'A'. The phone rang three times before his gruff voice blasted through my speakers.

"Gus, have you heard from, Assata? I've been trying to call him, I keep getting the voicemail? It's starting to worry me to be real."

I could hear him fumbling with something in the background before he said, "Naw, fam, last I heard from bro, he was making a run. You know dawg, though. I'm sure he's good. What's poppin' though, you need something done? You know all you gotta do is say the word."

I hesitated for a second or two this shit I was holding inside, wasn't the type of shit you just go blurting to just anybody, but this family. Gus been rocking with the circle since the sandbox. He had a right to know just as much anybody else. So, I told him what Kesha told me about the phone conversation, that was overheard. I even told him how Kesh said he ended the call.

Maybe he could help me piece this shit together. His side of the line was silent for a second before he said. "Where you at, Jazz? Don't be riding around the city looking for no mu'fuckin' killa by yo' self, wait on Assata. Where are you?" he fumed.

Before I could answer, my phone beeped alerting me that another call was coming through. I glanced and almost hung up on Gusto to answer Assata's call.

"Never mind, Gus," I said without waiting for a response.

***

~Six~

Assata just dropped me off at home. There were no more tears, but the hurt was still raw. I couldn't believe this nigga chose another bitch over, me. The bitch that rides with him no matter the situation. I asked myself a thousand times, what could she have over me? Was her pussy better, her head game? Was she prettier, freakier? What makes this shit so deep, is that he spit in my face even further, by dropping four rubber-banded bundles of money. He said it was forty grand and had the audacity to say, he didn't want to see me in the club again.

Really nigga? I left that shit right there in his car. I was lost as I entered my apartment. As soon as, I closed the door and locked myself in. I placed my back to the door and soft tears clouded my vision.

"I hate him, I hate him, so much," I whispered.

Sucking in a deep breath to calm my nerves something more than air erupted my lungs. The familiar aroma caused my stomach to drop.

I hadn't had a face to face with him in months. I'd ducked him all I could, but I knew eventually he would come. The red ember at the tip of the wineberry black-n-mild, he loved so dearly was the only indication, that he was sitting on my couch. It was so dark, I couldn't make out his features, but I didn't need light to distinguish his pretty ass. The nigga had been in my nightmares since I met him. With my eyes now adjusted to the darkness. I could see his silhouette moving as if he was a phantom of the night.

Suddenly, he was so close we could've kissed. "You can't answer the phone for a nigga now, Six?" He whispered against my lips.

Disgust swirled through me. "What do you want, dude?" I tried to push past him, but he forced me back in place and like magic, his fingers appeared around my neck. "I can't— can't—breathe." I rasped, scratching his hands.

Slowly he eased his grip, but his hand was still in place to remind me of the thin line between life and death.

"What do you want? I told you our business was over after the last time. I told you, I love Assata, but you steady try to use me to get at him. Why do you hate a man that would die for you?" I hissed, as my eyes got cloudy.

"Bitch, you don't know that, nigga! He's not who you think he is." His eyes flashed with a look of hurt. "He did this to me." he seethed.

Emotions was like a hurricane in him, as he released me and headed for the couch. I studied him, as he sat down and picked up the cigar.

"What did he do to you? That man is—" My words died as fresh pain reminded me what he'd done to me.

As if he could see right through the turmoil, forming a river within me, he said. "So, he finally told you 'bout his lil' slut, huh?" He laughed at his own humor. He'd warned me, I was about to get my heart broken, but love had me blind.

"Look, Six, we got a problem. It may benefit your situation, as well as get me closer to yo' goal, but—"

I put my hand up to stop him. "No, whatever it is, you can do it yourself. I told you, I want nothing else to do with this shit. I—I love that man regardless of who he's with." I mumbled.

He stood up and walked over to me. He placed his fingers under my chin, lifting my eyes to his. "Ma, it matters not how deeply you love him. If he finds out you had a hand in Shy's murder, he's gonna murder you in cold blood."

I frowned, "Wha—what?" My mental spun rapidly. How, does Assata know? Is that why he gave me the money—to leave?" A million questions danced in my head until he solved the riddle. "While you was playing in the sand—" he brushed the sand off of my chest. "His bitch has been playing private eye all over the city. At this moment, she's trying to find Shy's phone. If she does shit's gonna get real bloody. So, she has to go."

Fear raced through me. "I thought you said, there was no way this would trace back to us. You've used me ever since I met you and—" a knock at the door, caused him to place a hand over my mouth, silencing me. With the other hand, he pulled out his pistol.

I removed his hand and gently pushed him towards the back room. He resisted at first, but the sound of Assata's voice motivated him to take cover. I watched until he disappeared. The last thought I had, before turning back to the door was,

'Gusto is right if Assata finds out, I was part of his boy's murder—I'm a dead bitch.'

***

~ Assata~

"I know you're in there, Six. Open the door, baby girl." I'd been standing out there a good five minutes before I heard movement behind the door.

"What do you want, Assata? You said all, that you needed to say shouldn't you be home with your—your—what did you call her, your Earth?"

This is why mu'fucka's don't keep it solid with each other. The truth is always sought but rarely respected. Being a real nigga has lost its value, it has become a spoken identity. People have become too lax in faking with each other, that lying to the face of the ones they love have become natural. That's not how it goes.

My frustration mounted. "Six, look fam, I find it funny how you always telling me to keep it muddy with you. But, when I do, you shun my realism. How am I, supposed to respect you as a woman, if I can't even talk to you without the fear of you not respecting me for keeping it real?"

That must have done it because the door opened and she quickly stepped outside and shut the door. Her body language seemed fishy, but maybe I was trippin'.

"Damn, a nigga, can't even come in no more?" I laughed to kill the tension.

She leaned against the door and crossed her arms over her chest. Attitude strained her face and the redness of her eyes told me, she'd still been crying. I gotta weak spot for shorty, so this shit fucked with my two-step.

"Look, Six, I just came to give you this." I dropped the cake, I tried to give her earlier at her feet. "I know, you ain't no charity case. I ain't trying to pay you off, dawg. A nigga—"

She frowned, "Nigga, what I tell you about calling me your, fam? I'm not one of them niggas you trap with. I understand you got a new bitch or better, yet you've been having her around. I'm just the last one to know, but I'm gonna be respected. Call me by my name, Assata," she fumed.

I think I need to let mama cool off cause the way she rockin' wit' me, would make me fuck around and go upside her head, and she knew it. I stepped to lady and pulled her close to me. I wanted to kiss those juicy ass lips, but the respect I have for Jazz wouldn't let me play myself.

Was I wrong to feel for shorty? She kept it all the way funky with the God. Even though I was bred not to trust, she was one of the few people in this life that I did.

"Look at me, Six," I demanded. Her eyes bored into mine, as I prepared to make my exit. "You are a nigga's backbone. You've fucked with me even before the pennies and whips. I thug with you the long way, Ms. Lady. You gotta stand by me through my every decision—not just some of them." I wrapped my arms around her and pulled her closer to me. Her body was tense and there was something strange about her facial expression, that I couldn't quite put my finger on. I paid it no mind, as I slide my hand over the imprint of her pussy lips to emphasize my point.

"I'd never tried to lock down this pussy, nor have I prevented you from finding your sense of love. I've never experienced it—can't really say I believe it even exists. But, this shit I feel for lady, started way before you, and it has nothing to do with you." I took my hand and brush the loose strand away from her face. Will you be content with me seeing you fantasize? Would it have been better for me not to have told you?"

She shook her head, that one action caused her soul to leak from her eyes in an emotional thunderstorm. "I just—I love you, Assata. You've always known that. I know your just keepin' it 'G', but what about me? What do you expect me to do with these feelings I have, huh? While your somewhere playing house with some other bitch. What do you expect me to do? My heart is yours, Assata. I'm not able to see this shit, right now."

I held baby girl as I digested her words. I don't know if it was the moment, or if someone very close around was smoking Gusto's favorite Black-n-mild.

RENTA

Chapter Twelve
To Die For

~3 Weeks Later~

~Destiny~

I walked into the Golden Triangle Mall trying to be inconspicuous, as I headed for the food court. Man, I don't know why he chose this place to meet out of so many other places, that would've been less of a possibility of us being caught. The glasses I wore seemed to cover most of my face, and the shawl covering my head made me feel comfortable enough to walk without fear of being spotted.

I was elated to see that the court was clustered with people. I spotted the man, I'd come to meet at a corner table. He smiled and waved me over. The smell of hot pretzels and fried foods aroused my senses until my stomach reminded me, that I hadn't eaten all day.

"Hey, baby, how has your day been?" He greeted, with a warm hug before we took our seats.

"It's been a long one Sa'Mage. I just need it to be over with. As a matter of fact, I can't wait until all of the craziness is over and I can come back home." I interlocked my hand with his I hadn't felt his touch in months. "I yearn to sleep in my own bed, with my own husband. Is that too much to ask? Sa'Mage smiled, then released my hand, and returned his attention to his food. "I know you have enough on tape to convict, Ice-Berg and his brother ten times over. That man even admitted to kidnapping me. I've worn wire after wire!"

Sa'Mage swiftly snapped his head up and placed his finger against my lips, before gazing around the room to make sure no one overheard me.

"Keep your voice down, Destiny, you don't want anyone to overhear you," Sa'Mage said.

I nodded my head in understanding before saying in a much lower tone. "I've been there during drug transactions and conversations Berg has had with his suppliers. Damn, it's the feds, a person can get convicted off word of mouth. What else do you need?"

Sa'Mage continued eating his food as if I hadn't said anything. Okay, okay, I know you're wondering how did this come about? Well, the short version Sa'Mage is my husband, I love him. So, when he came to me with his plan to take Nutz and his crew down. I had reservations but once he assured me, he'd not only get his job back but also had a chance at becoming Governor of the state, it was a no-brainer. So, here I am his way of infiltrating Ice-Berg's circle. Never did we imagine, he would be in alliance with the kingpin Russia. A bonus so to speak.

"Earth to Destiny, what has your attention so deeply?"

Snapping back to the here and now, I tried to focus. "Huh, what you say?"

He smiled. "Are you thinking about your little boyfriend. Have you fucked him, Destiny?"

I was appalled. I'm out here risking my fucking life, for this stupid motherfucker, and he had the balls to question my loyalty.

"How dare you?" I sneered. "You have no fucking idea how hard it is to play a role for a man as dangerous as Nutz. At any moment, he can have the slightest hunch, and it will all be over. You are a fucking asshole, Sa'Mage." I stood up from the table and headed for the restroom.

On my way there I bumped into a brick wall, to my astonishment it came to life. "Excuse me—I am, so sorry!" I managed to say, as we both squatted to clean up the mess I caused.

"It's cool, lady, I shoulda been more aware of my surroundings instead of running my mouth on this phone. It's peace, my name's Assata, by the way—you are?" He extended his hand.

"She's taken," Sa'Mage said from behind me.

**

~Detective Hunter~

For the past few months, things have been tense. The massacre and discovery of, Bobby Ray a.k.a Brains, as well as his accomplice Snow, set off a bomb within the city. A lot of officials lost their jobs, and some were barely hanging on to theirs, due to us running an unauthorized task force. More importantly, this shit storm happened right under our noses. The pieces were still scrambled, but my guess is that the plan fell apart in the end. Somehow Russia caught on and killed Snow before slipping into the night.

The bad part is, we were blind to the slaughter until the gunshots from the .380 high point were fired. By then, death was already in the air and the house was clear. The director of the Bureau went apeshit. Now, I'm buried under a mountain of paperwork, as Detective Winslet poured me a hot cup of Java.

"What's the plan now, smart guy?"

Without looking up I said. "We're going to take them down regardless to what our superiors say. Once we get these scumbags in cuffs, we'll turn over the evidence we have and be fuckin—" the ringing of my phone paused me.

The text message that came through gave me great reason to smile. It's confirmed Nutz and Ice-Berg will be moving a shipment in three days from today, Saturday, February third.

***

~Jazzy~

I was so frustrated. Two weeks ago, we had our first real piece of hope, that would lead us to my brother's killer. Only to have it lost in a search for a phone, that has somehow vanished into thin air. My mom seemed to have thought I had it. Assata can't remember and Kesha won't answer her fuckin' phone. The night, I told Assata the story Kesha told me, he froze and stared. I told him the way she said Shy ended the call, he just couldn't wrap his mind around the possibilities.

"D.B.D." Is their circle's way of departing and only people close to them understands the depth of it. *'Death Before Dishonor'* is literal with the term. It narrows it down to two. It was absurd, because both him and Gusto loved Shy and would never harm him. So, someone was playing a dangerous game and it could only end one way—death.

Pulling up to Kesha's house, I felt a tingling feeling in my stomach. Don't ask me why, but shit was just too crazy, right now. I reached the door and knocked, on the second try the door crept open on its own. I glanced behind me, kids were out playing football in the middle of the street. Elders were out on their porches things looked normal. So, why did it feel like I was the white girl in the horror movie?

I laughed, as I pushed the door open and walked in. That's when I knew shit had got real. The stench was so heavy, I gagged. I covered my mouth and whether it was stupidity or sheer curiosity. I stumbled through the small house until I stopped where the smell was the strongest. The bathroom, I used my shirt to push the door open.

"There you are," I screamed in elation, seeing her smiling face.

That was until I saw all the blood spilling from both her wrists. Now I was screaming in horror!

***

~Ice-Berg~

Me and Nutz stood in the middle of this dusty ass warehouse, that used to be the old Morson Mills Factory before you entered the ghetto of Southeast Denton. You know, when shit is going too good for a nigga, some fuck shit always pops up. As my brother, smiled at the fifty bricks that had just been delivered. I wondered where did all this end for him.

With that in mind, I turned to him. "That shit looks like chow time huh, bruh?" I grinned at his excitement.

He turned to me, "Nigga, we here. This what we do it for." My eyes told a story of disappointment that he caught instantly. "Sup, fam? You got the world at your fingertips, but you looking like you don't deserve it."

I shook my head, as I leaned against the wall. "It's not that at all, cuz—it's just—maaannn, we can't sell dope forever. I mean, there has to be another plan, Nutz. Now, that we're at the point in life, we've always dreamed of we gotta have an exit."

I watched him sit down on an empty crate and pick up one of the kilos of raw cocoa. He pulled out a small pocket knife, cut a small slit in the tape, and scooped a small mountain onto it. I watched as my little nigga snorted this bullshit and leaned his head back as if he'd discovered that heaven ain't so far away.

When he finally set his eyes on me he said. "My nigga, you've always known this was the life for me. I've been having these street dreams our whole mu'fuckin' life. I am a dope boy, Berg, the game is all I know. I don't know the first thing about running no bidness, bro. I'd rather stay at what I know and bleed this concrete."

Anger rushed through me. I wanted my brother to see beyond his false sense of success. I slapped the brick out of his hands before I gave him my spiel. "Bro, ain't no future in what we do, fam. Yea, we know a few successful mu'fuckers in the game. That's because they branched out beyond the streets, or they quit while they was ahead."

I kicked the brick so hard, it slid across the floor leaving behind a white trail. "Nigga, damn near everybody we grew up with either dead or doing football numbers. None of them niggas coming home no time soon." I used my fingers to count the few homies we lost in the game. "Dino got thirty, T-money got close to the same shit, Lil' Tay caught forty-five, and Lil Red facing forty. Now, tell me, fam you see a happily ever after in them type of numbers? When the last time you wrote one of them, Nutz?"

My younger brother merely shrugged. "That's what I'm saying, folk, you forgot 'bout them niggas just like everybody else. Look, Nutz—I know what it feels like for them white folks to play God with your life. I don't give a fuck about how much a mu'fucka claims they love you. They'll leave you for dead. I love you to death and even if you was facing life, I'd never turn.

"Nutz, life don't stop our grief. Mu'fuckas ain't loyal no mo', fam. Every bitch you've ever given your heart to will be in the wind, the very minute you sign your name on that dotted line. I'm tellin' you, fam. Let's change the story, homie. Our book ain't gotta end—"

Nutz jumped up with anger registered on his face. "Look, big bruh—I ain't on this spiel you giving niggas. You want to know what your problem is, fam. You've become too big for where we came from. Bruh, you, my dude and I'll kill the world for you, but I ain't rocking how you rockin', right now."

Our eyes locked in a showdown of pride and finality. "Cool!" I said without looking away. "After this our road splits, bro. You're my other half and when you need me, I'll rise to the occasion, but let me pour you this last cup to sip from, family. Even Escobar was knocked down from his very own tip of the mountain. I ain't going back to that cage, Nutz. I've been behind that wall twice, you saved me once. I'm out before I'm crucified. After this I'll introduce you to, Russia— I'm out, fam."

***

~Six~

I never fucked Gusto—never. I met him a month before Shy was murdered. All four of them were really close. It surprised me when Gusto, showed up to the club by himself and paid me for a dance. I was hesitant he knew I was Assata's girl, and truth be told a bitch knew that nigga was foul and had I entertained him, I would've been just as sour as he was. So, I gave him his bread back and went on about my business, but when the doors closed and it was time to go home, there he was.

A pretty boy ass nigga with a bankroll, he tossed in my hands. It was so many big faces, I thought he was playing some type of game. Ain't no lap dance that expensive. The curiosity got the best of me and we ended up in his Rover, with him giving me his rundown on murkin' the nigga I saw

Assata with religiously. At the time, me and Assata had barely started rockin', but I didn't know Shy like that. He never spoke.

The one time I did try to be cool and speak, he took it as me flirting and told Assata to check me. That punk shit didn't sit well with me, so I concocted something real slick for his ass. Long story short, I had my homegirl, that danced with me lure him where Gusto told me to and from there it was a wrap. Then, after Assata did me dirty, I figured it was cool for me to start talking to Gusto. There was no better way to hurt a nigga than to fuck somebody he's close to.

Not long after we started kicking it, I was ready to put this wet pussy in his life. We were chilling at my place. We had been up all night taking shots and just kicking the shit. Just when my kitty started throbbing Gusto passed out on me.

'Ain't this some bullshit?' I said to myself.

Looking down at him, I decided to wake him up to some of this good pussy. Maybe if I got his nose wide open Assata would see what he's missing. I unbuckled Gusto's pants, reached down into his boxers and pulled his dick out. It only took a few licks and a stroke to get that motherfucker hard as steel. Easing down on him was delicious and as he stirred, my pussy was tight and wet. I rocked back and forth while pressing my hands down on his chest.

"You definitely know how to wake a nigga up." He said in a gruff voice, as he pumped the dick up to meet my grinding hips.

"You like it, boo?"

"Fuck yeah."

"Show a bitch, how much you like this fat pussy." I licked my lips in anticipation.

"Oh, I'm about to show you." he boasted.

Gusto flipped me over onto my back and stuck his face in my dugout. His tongue parted my lips and he gripped my ass tightly, as he searched for my clit. Before long I was humping that nigga's face with no reserve. Minutes later, I showered his mouth with my liquid pleasure.

"Ummm," he moaned savoring my taste. "Now, I'm about to blow your back out. Show you what boss dick feels like."

"Don't say it, *slay* it." I was dying to get fucked out.

I opened my legs as wide as I could and invited him inside my treasure. When that rock-hard dick penetrated me, I wrapped my legs around his waist and accepted all that he wanted to give me.

Gusto had me screaming with pleasure. As he pounded my pussy all I could think was, '*Damn, he got the typa dick that a bitch will die for*'.

RENTA

Chapter Thirteen
Gangsta's Cry Too

~Assata~

These past few days, I'd been trying to nurse my baby back to sanity. She'd never been any street bitch and too much pressure can burst the strongest pipes. I'd seen the toughest mu'fuckas snap under too much heat. The death of Kesha rocked mama. She'd been having some fucked up nightmares and some crazier mood swings. I hated seeing Jazz so vulnerable that's why I'd planned a night on the town with, Red. I'd even went, as far as doing something I hadn't done in years.

I'm in love with poetry, I'd been writing and displaying my work since I was a lil' nigga. It was just that, as shit got more time consuming, I hadn't had the time to expose that side of myself. I'm flying through the city collecting that bag. Shits been suave for the boy ever since the get down at the Russian's spot. The only thing that bothered me, was that shit had been too quiet. The calm before the storm, them niggas over there on Hickory and Oak Street been getting to that check as of late.

They'd took their hustle all the way up to Fred Moore Park, and that's too close to me, and my dawgs side of the hood. My villain niggas been barking at me 'bout a few run-ins with them niggas over making moves too close to the turf. Before I romance my lady, I gotta check in with my relative Lil' Joe to tell him to get his loc's in check before it's bloodshed. Joe was a hothead, he and his ace, Lil' Mack had never been scared to put their murder down, but that was my flesh.

At one point in time, we were thick as thieves. I came up sleeping on the same floor when Aunt Pearl used to let a nigga come in outta the cold. Even though, my fam was Crip crazy he loved me to death. Y'all fuck with me I'm gonna put it down for the real niggas tonight.

***

~Jazzy~

The sound of my phone ringing forced me from my bed, that had become my coffin. My girls had been calling me, for the past few days. I had yet to return a single text or call. Honestly, things had been mad crazy. You would think, that Shy being my brother and my attraction to hood niggas, would've prepared me for this kinda shit, but I'd never been a part of this typa lifestyle. So much blood, so much death. I just couldn't deal. While scrolling through my text, I noticed one from Nutz. Surprise surged through me it had been weeks. Even against my will, his message caused me to blush.

//: Sup, beautiful? I know shit has been crazy for you. I respect your stand, with your new dude. I'm not trying to disrespect that at all, but my heart wants you to know. I love you, regardless who we're with. Whether, you'll admit it or not, I know you still hold a special spot for ya' boy. I'm just sending you my love, queen. I'm Nutz over you!

Instinctively, I smiled but still erased it without a response. I'll always have love for Nutz but I'm not that type of female. My heart beat for 'A' and regardless of my history with, Nutz there was nothing in this world, that could make me hurt him like that. As I scrolled down, my alert went off telling me a picture message just came through. Nutz is crazy. I clicked on it, Nutz was cheesin' real hard, holding a giant bear and what seemed to be a bottle of wine. The caption underneath read.

Open up, I brought you brunch!

Confused, I read the text again. The sound of the doorbell scared me half to death. Looking down at my naked body, I rolled my eyes at the balls of this man. He knew Assata would snuff his lights out for disrespect, but he'd always been one to follow his own rules. It angered me, as I rushed to find something decent to throw on. Opting for some loose-fitting jogging pants and a muscle tee.

I headed for the door. Since my dad left the house to me before he moved to California. He never made any changes to this house, so this nigga could see me as I entered the living room. He grinned at me through the glass on the side of the door, as if he could care less that my posture was hostile.

"What the fuck, Nutz?" I was heated, as I swung the door open. "Fuck you just pop up at my house without being invited? You know, this ain't cool, my dude and before shit gets misconstrued, you need to leave."

Hurt registered on his face. "Look, ma, I'm not here to disrespect you or your man. Marcella just told me you've been lost since, Kesha eighty-sixed herself, and you not answering nobody's calls. I just came to put a quick smile on your face and dip. My gal' waiting on me anyway" he said.

My attention was drawn to a tiny whimpering noise at my feet and my heart was stolen, when I looked down at the white Pitbull puppy.

"Oh my, God." I stooped down to pick him up and that's all it took for me to fall in love with him. Hugging him close to me, I looked back at Nutz. "Thank you. I appreciate the love Nutz, you know how to make me smile—always have, but the fact still remains that this ain't how it go."

Nutz nodded his head in acknowledgment. "You've always been loyal to who you're with." His eyes were tainted with a question, he seemed to fight with. "Can I ask you a question, Jazz?" I nodded my consent. "Before you left, why'd you hurt a nigga, like that? Was it for, Assata?"

I smiled, that's been a million-dollar question for years. "No, Nutz, it wasn't for 'A', I just needed time to see life. You were and still are a die-hard street nigga. You wouldn't have been faithful. It wouldn't have worked. As far as, Assata, I've always G'd for him, but he wasn't feeling me. He valued my brother too much. When I came back it was only to find out about, Shy. As we all know, no one can control the affairs of the heart, sooo—" I shrugged my shoulders. "It's obvious."

I assumed him finally hearing the truth of my decisions before I left had given him closure. I swear, I could actually see the burden lift off him.

"That's what's good, Jazz. I thought—" His voice trailed off. "It don't matter what I thought. I just want you to know, I'm here for you, fam"

Finally, noticing the bottle he had gripped in his hands. I looked at him with a smirk. It was Moscato my favorite, he knew it.

Noticing my look he said, "Oh, this, I just thought it wouldn't hurt to have one drink for old times sake. Maybe you can give me some advice on this new woman in my life."

Uncertainty unbalanced me, I battled with my loyalty versus the innocence of showing my appreciation, for this nigga showing concern for my well-being. I looked at him, something in my gut told me to just decline, and end this episode that's been in rotation for far too long.

"Nutz, look, you know you'll always be the man, that has taught me most of what I know. I gave you my purity, nigga, but at the end of the day, none of that shit matters. I got what I've looked for, for that nigga I am ten toes flat. I salute you and yo' gal, maybe one day we can sit down and have that drink, but Assata will be present. There's nothing between me and you, nor will there be any moments alone. The implication is sometimes greater than the act. I won't crack the trust, between me and mine for a moment in time. I appreciate the gifts and concern, but after this, our road is at its end."

The look in his eyes was a mixture of hurt and pride. With a small smile, he sat the giant bear and bottle at my feet, before erecting himself and pulling me to him.

Kissing my cheek, he embraced me and replied. "You've always been a rare female, Jazzy. I respect your vibration, baby girl. I just wish I was the lucky man."

***

~Assata~

Whoever said gangsta's don't cry, is a mu'fuckin' lie. Tears bled in my eyes as I pulled away from the curb. I'd just pulled up to Jazzy's spot to check on her and got the surprise of my life. Nutz holding a big ass teddy bear and some wine— Jazzy smiling. My first thought was to jump out and whack they dumb asses, but the playa in me wouldn't let me go out like that. I've always stood by the reality, that a nigga can't control a hoe's pussy when it's her nature to be who she's always been. I can never blame the nigga for getting his dick wet if there's no loyalty, or brotherhood to be loyal to.

"Damn," I whispered as I blinked away the pain in my eyes.

First time, I'd ever given myself to a bitch, look what I get! I was speeding through traffic, replaying the vision of Nutz leaning in to kiss her before I smashed off. *Real niggas get raw deals!*

***

~Six~

I stirred in my sleep as the dream I was having became a nightmare. Assata saw me and Gusto at a club and the hurt on his face was so deep, that satisfaction boiled over in me. That is until the tears fell from his eyes, and his pain was so powerful, it became my own. It was so thick, that it snatched me right out of my slumber. To my surprise, the tears and hurt followed me right into consciousness. Why the fuck did I stoop so low? I tripped the fuck out, my mental was aflame, and all I could do was cry, as regret raged through me like a tidal wave.

"What have you done, Six? Why would you, Man?" Gusto mumbled, almost giving me a heart attack.

I'd forgotten he was here. My room was dark, as he sat on the edge of the bed and pulled on his black-n-mild. The illumination from my window had shadows dancing around us as my drapes drifted lazily in the wind.

"I—I don't know, Gus." Shame ate at me. "I just was so hurt, so confused—drunk, I—" Every excuse I came up with seemed empty.

The truth was there was no rationality for this sin but at the same time. I knew I couldn't take it back. Suddenly, I felt dirty.

"Gus—this was never 'pose to happen—none of it. You gotta go—our dealings are over. I'm telling Assata, every—" At the speed of lightning, he stood before me with a gun, so big it looked fake in his hand.

"Bitch, you ain't telling Assata, a fucking thang. You did this to yourself. Your dumb ass allowed your pussy to lead you to an early grave." The confused look on my face, allowed him to look at me in a way, that I could only describe as sympathy.

He sat down beside me, the story he told me rocked me to sleep. "Last night you asked why I hate, Assata, so much. Why I did, Shy in? Well, this is it. I tell you this because I'm a good nigga at heart. Six, life made me a monster. My own squad dug me an early grave and now you've written your own script in this horror movie. About three years ago, Shy called me and told me to get dressed. Him and Assata was on their way to pick me up 'cause they had a team of bitches that wanted to rock with us.

"One of the girls wanted me specifically and said the other two wouldn't move without their girl. My first response was naw, I'd been out in the Ruts all week. I'd promise my bitch it was her night. As a matter of fact, as I spoke to my dawgs my wifey was in the shower preparing to fuck me in every way I could imagine—anything I could fantasize 'bout. I had it right there in my own home.

"But naw—Shy, kept screaming this bullshit 'bout it's my turn to take one for the team, etc. So, I did what most street niggas do, I lied to my queen to show up for, my niggas. Make a long story short—" his face contorted, as he relived the worst night of his life.

I held my breath, as he cleared his throat and continued. "We get to this house on Ruth Street and the girl, that answered the door embraced, Shy. Some bitch named, Vodka. I won't lie, the little bitch was super thick, with a pretty face to match. So, you know, I could only hope my hounds blessed me as equally, rather than sticking me with the lil' sista that's bigger than the big sista." We both laughed at his humor.

I was still lost as to where he was going. But intuition told me, that at the end of this tale, I wasn't going to like his conclusion.

"To my surprise, the sista they introduce me to was the baddest one of the three. An amazon with so much ass, I assumed she had to have paid a bankroll for it. She introduced herself as, Da'Shana. She told me she'd had her eyes on me for a long time. She said we'd met a few months ago at Club Infernos and I never called her.

"That shit sounded funny, cause a nigga in my position can't afford to forget a face. Beyond that I don't drink, so the hoe had to be lying. That should have been my indication, to take my ass home, but I am only a man. I did mention, this bitch was bad with a capital 'B'. All in all, I fucked the hoe over and over again as my gal' blew my horn up. They say karma is a bitch.

"Not even two to three weeks later, me and my gal was maxin' at the spot when the news came on and there staring at us was the same bad bitch, I'd fucked with no condom. This bitch was wanted in three different states for passing along the virus. As I sat lost in a trance, my girl sucked her teeth, she couldn't have known, her next words would cause her—her life.

"See, that's why a mu'fucka gotta be careful, who they fuckin' with." She then playfully hit me in the arm and said, *"Baby, if you've fucked her you got that As-I-Die-Slowly."* She laughed, then I put two in her face!"

When he finished his tale my world spinned. It was like an outta body experience.

"So, now you know why I hate, Assata, so much. Why I put the fix on, Shy— and now, why you'll hate me so deeply! I got AIDS, Six—and I got it cause I thugged with niggas I loved to the dirt."

***

~Jazzy~

After Nutz left, I found a Hefty trash bag and disposed of his gifts, even the Moscato! The things a girl will do for love. Earlier, I got a text from Assata, that I must've missed when Nutz showed up.

//: *Don't be late. Meet me at Jhon-Jhon's at 9:10 p.m. sharp.*

10:15 a.m. December 3rd

Right up under that text was another one that confused me.

//: *I'm a block away—come outside!*

10:20 a.m. December 3rd

I don't know what made my heart race, but I look at the time of his text, and tried to remember what time I'd received Nutz text and erased it. My heartbeat was in overdrive, as I came up blank. I said fuck it and hit my baby up. I couldn't put my finger on it, but something wasn't right. If Assata said he was around the corner, why didn't he show up? Why didn't he call me this morning? Why ain't he pickin' up? By the time I concluded what musta happened, I was in a river of tears.

I'd called him ten times in the last twenty minutes and every time it went straight to voicemail. The puppy barked at me as if he knew something was up.

***

~Six~

"*AIDS!* I—gave—myself—AIDS!" It seemed to echo off the walls of my mind like a loud drum in an empty room.

I stood on shaky legs and so many emotions poured out of me. They boiled over into a fit of rage as I showered Gusto with blows. The guilt inside me thirsted to place the blame on anyone else, but myself.

"You did this to me," I screamed as he tried to restrain me.

Suddenly, I didn't know if I was lying down or standing up as stars circled in my head. I didn't understand what had just happened until Gusto stood over me with murder in his eyes.

"Look, bitch, I never intended to fuck you. I'd never fuck over nobody like that. It's only one mu'fucka, I want to feel my pain. Now, that you've committed suicide, I gotta way we both can get some revenge.

Chapter Fourteen
All Is Fair in Love and War

~Ice-Berg~

It's been almost three weeks since I turnt Nutz on to the plug and cut ties with the game. After the lick on Russia's bitch ass, things got spooky. Even though Russia hadn't said anything, I knew in these types of situations everybody was a suspect. I think the only thing that allowed me to still have life was the fact that, Snow was a white girl and there was no way to link her to me or my people. As a matter, of fact, those were the words from Belle's mouth.

She was still hot, that the murder plot turned out to be a robbery, that left everybody leaking, but the intended victim. I told her shit happens. Yeah, when shit has cooled off, we'll get his bitch ass, but right now he's running his operations from across the water. He had business with the big boss and he'd been M.I.A for a few weeks. I'd been running that dick in, Belle. That bitch is an animal in the bed. I know, I'm playing with fire, but how could I let this boss bitch get away, without seeing if what they said about Latin women is true?

It is her pussy wet as Niagara Falls, and she freakier than a porn star. I see why them ese's be putting all them babies in they women. They never stop fucking. It's now 9:15 p.m., I'm at the crib with so much to do. My doorbell let me know, my company had already arrived. Going to the door, I smiled in anticipation of this bitch.

Belle got a nigga nose open. As I opened the door, she pulled the sash on her coat, it opened and she was butt ball naked underneath it. See, this is why I got so much to do, but not enough time to do it.

***

~Jazzy~

Me and my girls sat at a table center stage. We were enjoying ourselves, as beautiful brothas and sistas showed their talent. I'd yet to hear from Assata. I just prayed that he'd show. I remembered him telling me, he does stand up poetry, but it's kinda hard to believe. I've only seen that other side of the man. Tonight, I hoped to not only get the opportunity to meet the other side of Assata, but also to see if my assumptions were correct, or if I was merely overreacting.

Someone nudging my shoulder snapped me outta my thoughts, just in time to hear some host introduce an Afrocentric Queen named Freedom to the stage. She stepped to the mic, as the lights dimmed, and the spotlight radiated her beauty. Her wild hair glistened from underneath a red scarf and her big Bambi like eyes were at half-mast, as she caressed the mic like it was the most beautiful dick she'd ever touched. The crowd simmered down, her beautiful full lips opened to reveal a deep sultry voice, that put you in that mood to make deep passionate love.

"Hey, Gods and Earths, I'm here again to do a piece that I call, 'Forever in a Glass Jar'. I know you sistas out there gonna feel me on this one. I just ask you brothas to vibe with me, as I give you me." She said as she turned her eyes to a midnight black brotha at the table next to mine.

"I wish that forever could be captured in a jar, held until we meet again. I don't know when that will be, but if it's in another lifetime I'd hand you the jar, and when you open it, we'd be transported back to this week again.

"During our last encounter, I vowed to never be weak again—

We argued—
We fucked—
And then you left as if we'd never speak again.
 But, every time, I closed my eyes I fell so deep again. I find no peace in merely 'I', or me, and him. I just thirst for 'we' again. Wait, there I go again—
Lusting for a love that's no good for me.
 I'm not saying, you're too hood for me. I'm just asking if you think, forever can be captured in a jar?
 I wonder, God, within everything that's been manifested, tried and tested.
 "Why can't you trust? I know the last woman you gave your heart to was a slut, but how can you hold her sins against me? Simply because she only knew how to love if you made her nut, but you'd simply thought she'd change cause you loved too much? Hush!
 I don't want no excuses, I'm not foolish enough to think a lifetime of pain will be erased overnight. But, the essence of a soldier's fight is what makes him reign supreme. There's no such thing as finding forever in a dream.
 "Just painted scenes captured on a canvas lost within a forest of trees.
 So, maybe we will meet again—it may be in another lifetime—at that moment, I'll embrace you warmly and tell you, that I understand now how knowledge and wisdom can give birth to a star.
 Even though, it's a beautiful fantasy, forever can't be captured inside of a glass jar—"

The room erupted, as she held up a clenched fist, and smiled her departure. The host held up a glass of cognac.

"Yeah, y'all had to feel my girl, Free. She always heats this muthafuckin' mic up." He hyped the crowd. There were snaps and glasses in the air all around the packed room. "Now, tonight, we have a special young brotha that's been more like a son to me over the years. Now, for those of you who ain't never experienced this shit before. Playas hold on to your la-dies, ladies hold onto your panties, cause my youngin' is gonna have to come on with it after what Free just did."

The crowd reacted to his test with a round of applause. "So, without further ado, y'all mu'fuckas show some deep love to my boy, Assata!"

Chills ran down my spine at the mere mention of his name. The lights dimmed, and a red spotlight shined down on the small stage. Anticipation was thick, as we all waited for his presence to fill the room. Me solely, I waited for our eyes to meet. Suddenly, he was there, center stage and shirtless. His chocolate skin stained with tattoos of his journey. The ski mask on his stomach was the biggest piece. It was a goon praying as chaos erupted around him.

His Gucci pants slightly hung from his waist only Assata could step into a club with his burna tucked in his waistband on full display. As sexy as this God was the one thing that couldn't be ignored, was the pain in his eyes. He pulled the microphone out of its cradle, with one hand and held a big Gulp cup that only those close to him, knew was filled with his drink of choice codeine, in the other.

"What's the bidness world? I had a piece that I worked on for the past few days. But, after the pill, I had to swallow to-day. I think I'll do my best shit giving it to you straight from the gut." Then as if he knew I'd come, as if he had this partic-ular seat reserved for me. He looked through the darkness and his eyes lock with mine. My assumptions became my reality. My heart crumbled into a million pieces as he cried internally.

"Shid after that heat, Free, just laid down. I didn't know if I'd be able to live up to the standard," he flashed his diamond smile at Free who was now sitting to my right. Some female in the back of the room screamed over the noise.

"Don't worry about the standard, suga, just give us your soul, just standing your sexy ass up there has me lost in your vibe."

The crowd roared in amusement. Assata nodded in appreciation, as he sat his cup down on the stage, and looked back in my direction.

"I'll call this one, '*Ocean of Grief*'.

At a time, that I had lost focus you appeared like hocus-pocus. Poetry in motion, I don't even think you know it.

I know, that this is my chance at true love, I don't want to blow it.

So, here, I'm giving you my heart and trusting you to hold it, cause I'm a good nigga from a city gone mad. Guess, I just fell in love with a good girl in a situation gone bad.

I wanna say this is the best thing I've ever had. Honestly, I ain't got nothin' to compare it to.

It's like, spending a few bands on a suit, but having nowhere to wear it to. Or like, you're a bag of money and I'm the poor man, that happened to stumble up on you. All I can do is stare at you—

Crazy, I guess—but today you taught me well.

An ocean of reality under a small ship, set to sail.

I wanna degrade you and call you names like slut— whore—or Jezebel, but how can I condemn you for not being who I wanted you to be. When you're just being a female?

"That would be like—like sayin' an oyster isn't an oyster simply because it's lost its seashell or losing my faith in a wish simply because none of mine has come true. Even though, I've dropped a penny in three wishing wells.

I wonder— if Superwoman ever fell weak, who would she be?

Would Coretta Scott King, still be legendary if she ever chose to cheat?

Would Martin still dream without sleep, or if I was a different typa nigga, would the love we have to be so deep, that I could see beyond this pain at my feet, that's drowning me in an ocean of grief?

"Yet, that's just what I wonder. I'm not the typa nigga, that can look back where I began. 'Cause at times it's hard to look through the rain and see the sun.

There's no way for you to be the moon without reflecting the sun. Now my moon lives behind an eclipse.

I speak to the Heavens until there's a hole in my chest big enough to sink three ships. It's as if my mental is at war with my heart, strapped up with three clips.

I'd be a lie to say, I am happy for you. In fact, I wish, I knew magic, so I could conjure up something tragic for you. That's only for the moment. Tonight, I'ma cry in the shower so my tears can blend in with imagined raindrops.

My heart is now locked away, you'll never be able to reenter it cause I found a way to change the locks."

***

~Ice-Berg~

"Coje Esta Panocha, Cojela," Belle moaned, as she rode this dick.

Her titties swung in my face as I spread her ass cheeks apart. I was making sure she got every inch of this eight and a half inches of meat. The pretty bitch was riding me so hard, it almost hurt, but the *almost* part didn't hold a candle to the sensations rushing through my dick every time the pussy swallows me up, so I allowed her to freak out.

"Chu ready, huh? Chu ready for me to cu—cum, Papi?" She moaned as she sat up straight and fucked a nigga to death.

She was in her zone and my shit was pulsating when the sound of a lighter disturbed our melody, a small flame illuminated the dim room. Maybe this hoe was so far into the moment of euphoria, she missed the telltale signs of something being amiss. The sound of her husband's voice snapped her crazy ass back to reality real quick. Throwing her to the side, I snatched the .40 from under the pillow.

"You know, my friend—te ting I've never understood about you race is that you greed." He whispered through a mouthful of cigar smoke.

His two henchmen aimed Mac-90's at us awaiting the signal to turn my California king into my death bed. I looked to Belle to see how she was taking the sudden turn of events. To my surprise, the silly hoe had a smirk on her face.

"Chu could at least allowed me to get me nut before chu rudely interrupted," she purred.

This bitch had lost her mu'fucking marbles.

"Look, Russia—this—this shit is all wrong, fam. I—"

"Shut the fuck up!" He cut me off. "I'm an important man, Mister Swanson, so it pays to know what goes on around me. I've done work for the Solntsevskaya Bratva, as well as many other outfits. I'm from the old country, it pays to be observative. Have you ever heard of the 'Vorovskoy Zakon?'"

Before I could tell the sucka fuck naw, he continued. "Of course, you know noting of the codes, I'm bound by. You've shown you're disrespect enough to show, that you honor noting. I've always known my dear, Belle, was a slut—whore! I was willing to overlook, that small detail in the name of business. You see, her father is a very important man in my dear city of Moscow. He is, or shall I say was the man that supplied me. The deals he gave me were worth far more to me than his worthless daughter, he forced me to marry in order to reach such great success."

Belle began to climb outta bed at the past participle that he used in reference to her pops, but I blocked her with my arm. Hoe may be a human shield in a few seconds.

"Reno," He snapped, at the brute to his left. Instantly, he turned and walked outta the room.

"I no need the services with Mr. Chavez any longer. I've decided to cut—ummm?" He put a finger to his head as if he was in deep concentration. At that moment, the nigga Reno came back with a black bag in his hands. Reaching inside, he pulled out a severed head. A sick feeling swirled through my gut, as the silly mu'fucka tossed it onto the bed, and I watched it roll until it was facing us with white eyes.

Simultaneously two things transpired. I leaped from the bed squeezing the tool, shid if I'm going out. I may as well do it like a 'G'. Pain exploded in my shoulder as I fell to the floor, the last thing I heard before the deadly silence was Belle screaming.

"Mi Papa," I guess Russia cut ties with the homie, literally.

Chapter Fifteen
When It All Falls Down

February 3

~Detective Hunter~

I sat at my desk as my mind ran wild. Tonight, was the night, that we take Ice-Berg and his flunky's down. There was no question in my mind, once we captured the pawns, they would give us the king on a silver platter. Russia wouldn't know what hit him, once the birds got to singing. We'd got a thirty-man indictment starting from the big man all the way down to the driver of his car.

'It's gonna be a beautiful night.' I thought when an officer I allowed to help with tonight's extravaganza interrupted my train of thought.

"Hey, Hunter, you think this prick of an attorney's wife knows what she's doing? Can she be trusted?"

I moved too quickly and knocked over my cup of Java, as I snatched him by his lapels. "Look, you fucking dickhead, what did I tell you about—" All eyes were on us.

I released him, smoothed the wrinkles I caused out of his thrift store jacket, and tried to calm myself. Lowing my voice I growled, so only he could hear me. "Listen, Sampson, this thing we going on isn't anybody's business. You can't just go around speaking as if this shit is public information."

I followed his eyes to something behind me, I locked eyes with Winslet as she stared at me quizzically. "Code blue," she said.

That's the code that let me know shit was about to get real peculiar.

***

~Six~

I'd been laying in my bed crying so hard I was sick. AIDS—HIV, that shit didn't happen to bitches like me. The pain had turned into seething heat, as I thought about the plan, Gusto ran by me. His logic was that if it wasn't for Assata neither one of us would be in this current predicament. Which was true in a sense, because if Assata wouldn't have called on Gus', to ensure he got some ass. Gus would have stayed home that night, instead of finding himself laid up in some infected pussy. If he wouldn't have tried to play me to the left like some sideline bitch, I wouldn't have fallen victim to a sick dick.

Assata has to pay for his role in this, I think a taste of his own medicine will be a perfect conclusion to this madness. That was my thoughts as I dialed his number to put me and Gusto's plan in motion. I would have never guessed how easy this would be until I heard the slur in his voice when he answered the phone.

"Assata, please come over, baby. I need you sooo badly." I cried into the phone.

He told me he'd be here and not to be on no bullshit before he hung up in my face. I glanced over at Gusto smiling wickedly.

"You may as well get over here and ride this dick one time before he comes. It can't do no more harm than it already has."

I'm a fool, but not no damn fool. I stood up and laughed at him. "Nigga, that's overkill. I wouldn't fuck you again if your dick ejected the cure to this shit. Assata is on the way, you need to leave."

***

~Nutz~

I'm heading out the door and without paying attention I run right into Destiny.

"Whoa—whoa, where you headed in such a hurry?" She asked, wrapping her arms around my neck.

I leaned down to kiss her pretty lil' lips then replied, "I got some shit to tend to, ma. I'm gone catch up with you in traffic. You're welcomed to stay until I come back," I said dangling my keys in her face.

She looked at me strangely but quickly tried to cover it up with a smile. I caught it and curiosity had gotten the best of me. "What was that look for?"

She tried to front on the kid. "Nothin', baby, just get at me when you through with what you gotta do."

"What's the bidness, ma? You trying to slide with a nigga or sumthin'?" I went against my better judgment.

I'd already told her about my dealings and my plans, but I understood the nature of a woman. She'd walk into hell with a nigga if she rocked with him like that.

It's just the knowledge of knowing she's with him, that makes her disregard the danger of the mission. Since I locked in with shawty, she'd never been the type to crowd a nigga. It had to be the feelings, that had her looking at me as if I was lying to her.

"Why would I want to go with you to see another woman? Who you taking me for, Nutz?"

I studied her. *'Oh, that's what this is, she jealous. She all in her feelings 'cause she think I'm all up on the next bitch.'*

"Mama, you on some rah-rah shit, talking 'bout another bitch. You the only bitch I'm checking for, love."

197

She rolled her eyes and poked her lips out in a cute lil' pout. "Yeah, whatever—you can only try that, with one of those other little girls you be spending time with. I may be from the suburbs, but that doesn't mean I'll fall for that slick stuff you be trying to butter me up with."

Fire was in my eyes, I exposed queen. "You catching feelings, ma? Look, you know, what I do out here. Today I'm gonna be as dirty as I've ever been. To top it off, my brother has left the business to me. I don't want you being a part of this side of my life, but shid, I could use the company."

Peace washed over her features. Little did I know Berg's words would soon be the headline of my life. In my case, in order for two people to keep a secret between them, one of us had to be dead.

***

~**Assata**~

My mind was everywhere as I pulled up to Six's apartment complex. The drank I'd been taking to the neck, had a nigga lazy and the imbalance of today's events wouldn't stop playing on the big screen of my mental. This the reason why I keep my heart silent. When a nigga allows himself to feel for anything other than his bread, he becomes a victim to what he wanted to believe in, versus the shit he's always known.

I've always found it funny to see niggas falling head over heels for a bitch, expecting her to be the perfect hoe, but never thinking that before he met her, she was tainted. So, when she trips and falls on the next nigga's dick, why would you blame her? Calling her hoes and sluts, as if she didn't know that already. Her and her homegirls sit around and laugh about being sluts, but nigga's sit around and slap each other on the back for being suckas.

Shame on me. Sliding from the whip I only had two things on my mind—fucking the shit outta Six and this nagging feeling, I'd had in my gut ever since Jazzy told me what Kesha said. The nigga that killed Shy was on the home team. It was only one other mu'fucka that sealed a deal with the motto— but damn it can't be—

***

~Gusto~

Some niggas understood, why I rocked the way I rocked. Some were whispering behind my back, *"This is a hoe ass nigga!"*

They couldn't judge me, because they had never walked in my size tens. Yeah, I whacked, Shy. He had to know the hoe had that shit! How else could he explain me getting the baddest hoe in the house? Even, if he didn't know, him and Assata was 'posed to be my ride or dies. We'd put niggas in the dirt together. We lied, stole, and killed for the circle, *'D.B.D'—Death Before Dishonor!*

But, yeah, I wanted Assata to hurt, just as bad as I had been hurting the past few years. I wanted him to feel what he'd done to me. That's why I camped outside Jazzy's spot. She was too dangerous. The bitch was like a hound dog, and that's something I couldn't let ruin my plans. She'd been home for the past thirty minutes. I planned to wait outside 'till the lights went out, then make my move. Baby girl was about to sleep eternally!

***

RENTA

~Six~

Assata's eyes were intense as he stood in the doorway. I
could tell he was lifted, I could also see something else in him,
that I couldn't quite put a title to. A wounded animal maybe.

"You gonna let me in, or just stand there and stare at me,
fam?"

I hate when he referred to me as fam, my nigga, or any of
that shit he called his boys. I stepped to the side anyway, but
not before I gave him that look, he knew all too well. I watched
as he sat down on the couch. Then I closed the door and followed suit. My nerves were shot and the love I had for this
nigga was kicking my ass as I focused on his black ass.

"Was it his fault? Did he deserve what I was plotting to
give him? Why does it feel like this?" Questions danced in my
head. I tucked my feet underneath me, as I turned to face him.
That's when the power of this man hit me. Tears well up from
somewhere deep in him and raced down his face. He turned to
me and contradicted everything I'd convinced myself to believe was just and rational.

"Six—all my life, I never believed in happily ever afters.
I've lived to die and really never giving a fuck what comes in
between. I've never actually given a fuck about love or affairs
of the heart, cause to me loyalty died in the early centuries.
I—" he lowered his head and tried to compose himself.

Something about his pain washed over me, and his tears
became my own, as my eyes swam behind a threatening wa-
terfall.

"My moms was taken from me when I was fourteen. It's
like, God, played a bad joke on me. February fourteenth, she
asked me to be her Valentine. That was the last I knew of real
love because she was found D.O.A in an alley in Florida on

February fifteen, twenty-four hours later. Twenty-four hours, fam. I vowed to never give my heart again." he whispered.

Confusion turned into liquid heat as it dawned on me, that this nigga was sitting her crying over another bitch. I don't know if that's what pushed me over the edge or naw—fuck that. That's what I did, leaning over to him, I lifted his head up. First, using my tongue I licked his tears away, then climbed in his lap exactly like I did Gusto. I kissed his wanting lips. Maybe he wanted it, as bad as I wanted to give it to him, cause he kissed me back as if this was the reason he came here in the first place.

I reached down to undo his belt, as I grinded my pussy back and forth on his rigidness. His power strained against the fabric of his jeans and as I released him. I was thinking just like one of those vindictive bitches. Who'd been hurt by a nigga she loved too much, to see him happy with the next bitch. If I can't have him—well, y'all know the rest!

***

~Detective Hunter~

"Falcon one—this is team, Red Bear. Do you copy?" I said into my radio.

Me and my special task force had the road blocked off from Lakey all the way to Park Lane. We had the streets cornered off. Standing beside me was none other than the man, that made all of this possible former Assistant District Attorney, Sa'Mage! I told him it was a bad idea for him to show his face, but I couldn't argue with the fact, his wife was our star witness and was currently the passenger in the brown Crown Victoria we were waiting to appear.

"We copy Falcon One—we have the suspect in sight. He'll be your way in 5—4—3—2—"

***

~Nutz~

"Oh my God, Nutz, look at all these fucking police!" Des' screamed.

It seemed as if a million law cars had blocked off the road. I slowed the car to a stop. For some odd reason, something smelled fishy. As I sat there with D.P.D now blockin' me in from the back as well. All I could hear was Berg telling me, it's no future in this shit.

"Damn, cuz,' I said aloud.

Destiny seemed on the verge of panic, as she focused her vision on something in the distance. Her body language was odd, as I followed her eyes to what had her attention, my blood froze, and the pieces fell into place. The night I kidnapped her played in my mind, as if it was a motion picture.

"Where is my wife, you son of a bitch? I don't possess anything of yours and if it's money that you want—" he hissed into the phone on that cold night.

That memory was overshadowed by the scene at the art gallery the night Snow met Russia for the setup. I recollected passing a group of men. De Ja Vu made love to all my senses as I recalled seeing the familiar face. When I turned around to see the bidness one of the cats had disappeared in the night. Demonic laughter escaped my lips as reality slapped me dead in the face.

This hoe got one up on the kid. Not only me but nine times out of ten the hoe wired up, so the whole circle got a cell with their name on it.

"Nutz," she screamed. "Are you fucking kidding me. Are you about to try and shoot it out with the fucking D.P.D and F.B.I?"

Dazed, I looked down to find the grey and black Ruger clutched in my right hand. Truthfully, I couldn't remember grabbing it. I had ten bricks of raw in the secret compartments of this bitch, a loaded pistol, and the bitch that set me up. That was damn near life. I slapped the steering wheel in regret. My greedy ass dry riding to make a sale. I got workers for this shit. I just decided, that the twenty-minute ride to the spot would be easy money never could have anticipated this.

"Mr. Swanson, this is, Detective Hunter. We have you surrounded—there's no way out. Please, turn the car off and drop your keys and weapons out of the window."

I vaguely heard the cock sucka speaking through the bullhorn, as I hit the master lock to all my doors.

Destiny looked over at me bewildered as if to say. *"What the fuck"*, but instead she said, "Nutz, what all do you have in this car?"

Without replying, I reached into my pockets and pulled out the half ounce of snow, I kept on deck—just in case. I wasn't no junky, I just liked to get my nose dirty every once in a while. I poured a little mountain in the palm of my hand and did as much as I could before potency rocked my world. Destiny was disgusted.

"What the fuck are you doing? I can't believe you. You're worried about getting high, we have the whole state against us."

I merely leaned my head back and allowed my shit to drain. Feeling the last bit crawl down my throat, I looked over at lady, easing the tool to her face. I smiled menacingly, all the while the bullhorn was screaming *'bout this being my last chance at a peaceful surrender'*. He must not know my get down.

"Bitch take off yo' mu'fuckin' shirt." I hissed, as blood starting leaking from my nose. I was high as Pluto.

"Huh, take off my shirt? W—what are you talking about, Nu—Nutz?" she stammered.

My trigger finger was itching, I glared at the bitch. She couldn't know she was seconds away from her pretty face being knocked through the back of her mu'fuckin' head.

"No more games, bitch. I know you set me up—I see your husband out there. I know he was at the art gallery that night. So, dig, either you're about to do what the fuck, I ask you to do, or I'ma 'bout to knock yo' lips off your face. I won't ask again!" By now, the taste of blood let me know, I must have looked like an animal.

She must have seen the beast in me cause the fake bitch started blubbering 'bout them making her do it. She didn't want to—blah—blah—blah, so I did what my heart told me to do and slapped the slut in the mouth with the pistol.

The weak hoe's light turned out on impact, stupid bitch! I reached over and ripped the buttons off her shirt until the thin wire taped to her body was revealed—shit was funky now, my nigga!

***

~Jazzy~

I'd just finished cleaning the house from top to bottom. Now I was just tidying up my pops old room. I couldn't believe it was only a few years ago, that me and Shy would sneak in here and steal a few dollars from my pops stash. 'Till this day I think he knew we were stealing it, so he'd put more each time. He loved us and knew Shy was too stubborn to accept anything from him, so it was his way of catering to Shy's ego indirectly, anyway.

This man left half of his clothes some with price tags hanging from them, as well as his shoe collection. I smiled, as I walked to the back of the huge walk-in closet that's when I saw it. A clear bag with *'personal property'* stamped onto it. Instantly, I recognized the blood on the clothes inside it. My heartbeat was crazed, as I bent down to pick it up.

Tears blurred my vision, as I inspected the contents of the bag. I missed him so much. Preferring to put the bag back where I found it, rather than deal with the pain it was causing. I did just that, but before I could turn to walk away, a sense of nausea hit me. *The phone—could it be?*

Rushing back to the bag, I picked it up in my anticipation, I ripped it open. My brother's bloody clothes, jewelry, and a wad of money tumbled to the floor, but no phone. Rummaging through the bloody mess, it was as if Shy was urging me to keep going.

The jeans were stiff with blood, but even without the stiffness, there was no mistaking the imprint visible through the jean pocket. My pulse had reached my ears, as I reached in the pocket and my hand came in contact with the only piece of evidence leading me to my brother's death. As I pulled it out my hand shook. Without a second to waste I powered it on.

"Please, be charged," I begged to no one in particular, but maybe someone was listening because it powered on even though the percentage showed one-percent.

I anxiously awaited the call log to appear. As I waited, the notification flashed letting me know the battery was about to die. The call log appeared, my blood froze, the phone died and—

"You just couldn't let the dead rest huh, sis?" He said from behind me.

I knew I'd come to the end of my life. Honestly, the only regret I had was that I wouldn't be able to assure my baby, I died a real bitch.

***

~Assata~

I sat there on the couch, ass naked sucking the shit out of Six's titties. My drank had me sideways and I was numb. This bitch had been trying to get my dick up for the past half hour. She'd tried sucking it, jacking it, everything but put me in the pussy. As good as mama was lookin', my mind couldn't stop recapturing my bitch hugged up with my enemy. That shit rocked me. This that once in a lifetime typa bitch. This ain't how it 'pose to go.

"Assata," Six moaned in frustration.

"Huh, my fault baby girl I'm lost in the sauce."

Six jumped up with attitude and strutted her lil' sexy ass to her room. I could really care less, but right when I decide to get my black ass up and leave she came back and dropped to her knees. I stared down at her through hooded eyes, as she took my limp dick into her mouth, on contact something felt different. Six had my shit real wet and once she came off it with a popping noise, she blew softly and like magic, my shit saluted.

She smiled and pushed a halls cough drop to the front of her lips before swallowing it whole. She climbed back into my lap with the swiftness of a cat. She leaned down and stroked the dick, as she positioned herself above me. She placed soft kisses on my neck and paused before she inserted me.

"Assata—" she whispered between kissing my neck.

I turned my head, so she could do her thing, my eyes focused on something on the end table, that rocked me hard as fuck. As soon as her pussy lips began to kiss the head of my dick, I locked eyes with her. My high was blown. Shit started flippin' in my head like a horror movie. The aroma of the wineberry black-n-mild, I smelt the other day. I knew only one mu'fucka that smoked them, that damn sho' wasn't, Six!

'What the fuck!'

To Be Continued...
Who Shot Ya 2
Coming Soon

Submission Guideline.

Submit the first three chapters of your completed manuscript to ldpsubmissions@gmail.com, subject line: Your book's title. The manuscript must be in a .doc file and sent as an attachment. Document should be in Times New Roman, double-spaced and in size 12 font. Also, provide your synopsis and full contact information. If sending multiple submissions, they must each be in a separate email.

Have a story but no way to send it electronically? You can still submit to LDP/Ca$h Presents. Send in the first three chapters, written or typed, of your completed manuscript to:

LDP: Submissions Dept
Po Box 870494
Mesquite, Tx 75187

DO NOT send original manuscript. Must be a duplicate.

Provide your synopsis and a cover letter containing your full contact information.

Thanks for considering LDP and Ca$h Presents.

Coming Soon from Lock Down Publications/Ca$h Presents

BOW DOWN TO MY GANGSTA

By **Ca$h**

TORN BETWEEN TWO

By **Coffee**

BLOOD STAINS OF A SHOTTA **III**

By **Jamaica**

WHEN THE STREETS CLAP BACK **III**

By **Jibril Williams**

STEADY MOBBIN

By **Marcellus Allen**

BLOOD OF A BOSS **V**

By **Askari**

LOYAL TO THE GAME **IV**

By **T.J. & Jelissa**

A DOPEBOY'S PRAYER **II**

By **Eddie "Wolf" Lee**

IF LOVING YOU IS WRONG… **III**

LOVE ME EVEN WHEN IT HURTS

By **Jelissa**

DAUGHTERS OF A SAVAGE **II**

By **Chris Green**

SKI MASK CARTEL **III**

By **T.J. Edwards**

TRAPHOUSE KING **II**

By **Hood Rich**

BLAST FOR ME **II**

RAISED AS A GOON **V**

By **Ghost**

ADDICTIED TO THE DRAMA **III**

By **Jamila Mathis**

LIPSTICK KILLAH **III**

By **Mimi**

WHAT BAD BITCHES DO **II**

By **Aryanna**

THE COST OF LOYALTY **II**

By **Kweli**

SHE FELL IN LOVE WITH A REAL ONE

By **Tamara Butler**

LOVE SHOULDN'T HURT

By **Meesha**

CORRUPTED BY A GANGSTA **II**

By **Destiny Skai**

WHO SHOT YA II

By **Renta**

Available Now

RESTRAINING ORDER **I & II**

By **CA$H & Coffee**

LOVE KNOWS NO BOUNDARIES **I II & III**

By **Coffee**

RAISED AS A GOON I, II, III & IV

BRED BY THE SLUMS I, II, III

WHO SHOT YA

BLAST FOR ME
By **Ghost**
LAY IT DOWN **I & II**
LAST OF A DYING BREED
BLOOD STAINS OF A SHOTTA I & II
By **Jamaica**
LOYAL TO THE GAME
LOYAL TO THE GAME II
LOYAL TO THE GAME III
By **TJ & Jelissa**
BLOODY COMMAS I & II
SKI MASK CARTEL I & II
By **T.J. Edwards**
IF LOVING HIM IS WRONG…I & II
By **Jelissa**
WHEN THE STREETS CLAP BACK I & II
By **Jibril Williams**
A DISTINGUISHED THUG STOLE MY HEART I II & III
By **Meesha**
PUSH IT TO THE LIMIT
By **Bre' Hayes**
BLOOD OF A BOSS **I, II, III & IV**
By **Askari**
THE STREETS BLEED MURDER **I, II & III**
THE HEART OF A GANGSTA I II& III
By **Jerry Jackson**
CUM FOR ME

CUM FOR ME 2

CUM FOR ME 3

An **LDP Erotica Collaboration**

BRIDE OF A HUSTLA **I II & II**

THE FETTI GIRLS **I, II& III**

CORRUPTED BY A GANGSTA

By **Destiny Skai**

WHEN A GOOD GIRL GOES BAD

By **Adrienne**

A GANGSTER'S REVENGE **I II III & IV**

THE BOSS MAN'S DAUGHTERS

THE BOSS MAN'S DAUGHTERS II

THE BOSSMAN'S DAUGHTERS III

THE BOSSMAN'S DAUGHTERS IV

A SAVAGE LOVE **I & II**

BAE BELONGS TO ME

A HUSTLER'S DECEIT I, II

By **Aryanna**

A KINGPIN'S AMBITON

A KINGPIN'S AMBITION **II**

I MURDER FOR THE DOUGH

By **Ambitious**

TRUE SAVAGE

TRUE SAVAGE II

TRUE SAVAGE **III**

DAUGHTERS OF A SAVAGE

By **Chris Green**

A DOPEBOY'S PRAYER
By **Eddie "Wolf" Lee**
THE KING CARTEL **I, II & III**
By **Frank Gresham**
THESE NIGGAS AIN'T LOYAL **I, II & III**
By **Nikki Tee**
GANGSTA SHYT **I II &III**
By **CATO**
THE ULTIMATE BETRAYAL
By **Phoenix**
BOSS'N UP **I , II & III**
By **Royal Nicole**
I LOVE YOU TO DEATH
By Destiny J
I RIDE FOR MY HITTA
I STILL RIDE FOR MY HITTA
By **Misty Holt**
LOVE & CHASIN' PAPER
By **Qay Crockett**
TO DIE IN VAIN
By **ASAD**
BROOKLYN HUSTLAZ
By **Boogsy Morina**
BROOKLYN ON LOCK I & II
By **Sonovia**
GANGSTA CITY
By **Teddy Duke**

RENTA

A DRUG KING AND HIS DIAMOND I & II

A DOPEMAN'S RICHES

By Nicole Goosby

TRAPHOUSE KING

By **Hood Rich**

LIPSTICK KILLAH **I, II**

By **Mimi**

WHO SHOT YA

BOOKS BY LDP'S CEO, CA$H

TRUST IN NO MAN

TRUST IN NO MAN 2

TRUST IN NO MAN 3

BONDED BY BLOOD

SHORTY GOT A THUG

THUGS CRY

THUGS CRY 2

THUGS CRY 3

TRUST NO BITCH

TRUST NO BITCH 2

TRUST NO BITCH 3

TIL MY CASKET DROPS

RESTRAINING ORDER

RESTRAINING ORDER 2

IN LOVE WITH A CONVICT

Coming Soon

BONDED BY BLOOD 2

BOW DOWN TO MY GANGSTA

CPSIA information can be obtained
at www.ICGtesting.com
Printed in the USA
LVHW010828070119
602984LV00004B/415/P